Blurb

Loosely based on a true story. After being widowed in the second world war, Young School teacher Judith moves to start a new life in a remote Norfolk village (Hevingham). Finding herself alone in her remote cottage for long evenings she often finds herself talking to an old photograph of a young girl that came with the house. When the girl begins to haunt her dreams Judith becomes involved in a terrifying and jumpy ghost story.

Edited by Ann Attwood

About the author

Born in Norwich England in 1985 I grew up in the Norfolk broads.

I'm a qualified personal trainer, I've also worked at three petrol stations and in catering at Norwich City FC, but now working as a carer for disabled family members and writing in my spare time.

I have a sporting background, I won the English lightweight indoor rowing championship five times between 2005 and 2009 before having to retire through illness.

I grew up as a sea scout leader's son and have been a Sea scout leader since I was sixteen. I teach both Kayaking and Sailing.

I am married and I have stepchildren all in their teens.

I'm currently a season ticket holder at my boyhood club Norwich City.

Subscribe to my Website, Facebook and YouTube channel with these links.

Author's Website   samjwhite9.wixsite.com/samuel-j-white-books

Author's Facebook Page Author Samuel J. White | Facebook

Author's YouTube Channel Author Samuel J White Reviews indie authors

Maria's Photograph

Look out she's always watching you

Samuel J White

Copyright © 2019 by Samuel J White

All rights reserved.

No portion of this book may be reproduced in any form without written permission from the publisher or author, except as permitted by UK. copyright law.

Contents

Author's note — 1
1. Mary sits a weeping — 3
2. A frosty welcome — 7
3. The headmaster — 10
4. Not so Jolly farmers — 14
5. The farm by the lake — 18
6. The horse and cart — 21
7. Miss Spelling — 25
8. Thomas and his friend — 34
9. The Smith's farm — 39
10. The family photograph — 46
11. Nightmares — 54
12. End of term — 58
13. A family Christmas — 63
14. Cowboys and classrooms — 67
15. Back to school — 74
16. Goodbye Mr Robinson — 77

17.	A meeting from hell	80
18.	Hidden wounds	88
19.	Revelations	96
20.	Time to go home	100
21.	The Scrabble board	104
22.	A drink with Jerrold	110
23.	Jerry Smith	116
24.	The reall Maria	119
25.	The winter of 47	122
26.	A child in the school	127
27.	Alone in the dark	130
28.	The other photograph	135
29.	Mary	140
Epilogue added in 2017		143
Also By Samuel J White		147

Author's note

This book was originally published in late 2019 with the name of the village changed to hide it's identity. However, since then many people have come forward saying that they remember the real photograph on which this story is based.

It was as a very young boy in the early 90's when I was first made aware of the tail of a photograph, which had once been in a classroom at Hevingham Primary school. Legend said the girl in the photograph could make the desks move. Some say that her picture would move, and her eyes would follow you around. This story was passed down to the younger siblings of those who saw her long after she was removed.

Some sources say that the photograph was removed by the new head teacher in the late 1980's. Since writing this story, I have learned more about the photograph and heard varying accounts from people who remember it.

Years after she was gone, do to my mum working at the school, during weekly staff meetings I would be left alone on the school grounds. Despite the photograph being long gone, I could feel a presence watching me. Much of her legend is lost to time. One thing in the many stories remains consistent. She was a child who wanted to attend school but couldn't, possibly due to her death. In every story her name was Maria.

The story I have written is a work of fiction based on the rumours and the idea of exploring the origins of Maria and her photograph. All characters are a work of fiction although some may have similarities to real people.

I remain interested in finding out the identity of the real Maria and learning her true story. But for now, I would like to dedicate this work of fiction to the real Maria.

Mary sits a weeping

The eyes that looked back at me from the mirror were not my own. I shrieked and shook in surprise as they seemed to pierce my mind. The familiar face of the as-yet-unknown child spoke to me almost telepathically. She said only one simple phrase, but it stuck in my head like glue. 'Mary has found her playmate.'

I opened my eyes to the darkness. Beads of sweat ran down my face. Heart thumping in my chest. Where was I? Unable to see, I felt and searched the bed for my husband so he could comfort me, but there was no sign of him. Feeling my way along the wall, I found the light switch and flicked it on. It flickered into life with a crackle and I found myself in a small dark room with nothing but a bed, wardrobe and dressing table.

I took a moment to engage my brain and realised that I was in my new home. It was a new start, a new job, a new place too, and a new way of life. A new way of life without my husband, but then sadly, I rarely got a chance for a life with him when he was there.

Something was making a noise. A slow and haunting tune. 'Poor Mary sits a-weeping.' It came from a small music box on the dressing table. I remembered now that I wound it up to try and help myself drift off to sleep. It had now run down and was making the tune slow and eerie, causing my skin to quiver.

My only company that night came in the form of two photographs. One was my husband, the other was a faded photo of the strange nameless child. It was that nameless child that had just visited me in my sleep. Her eyes looked as if she stared at the camera. It was like she had some sort of illness, but without knowing her history, I could not make a valid guess at what it was.

It was the sight of her face in the mirror that had woken me from a dream. I had been on a farm by a lake. I had the music box, the same one that played the tune which I had awoken to. It was my favourite tune because I could relate to Mary and her lack of a playmate. I was not allowed to play with other children because I was doing differently from them. It had been a peaceful yet sad dream, harking back to a childhood that was not mine, as we often did. What had awoken me in such a sweat was the sight I saw when I investigated the mirror of the music box. It was not my face; it was *her* dream.

It was no wonder that I had dreamed about her with her photograph by my bed. Like her, I was very afraid of something. As my eyes adjusted to the light, hers in the photograph met with mine in the world of the living, as though she was trying to tell me something. I had somehow spilt a box of matches across the dressing table under her frame. The matches had fallen in such a way that they spelt out a single four-letter word.

'HELL'

Pretty frightening right?

So who was the girl? Why did I have her photograph? And why was she by my bed?

***

My new home came with my new job. When I opened the country cottage I was to call home, she was sat in her frame on the kitchen table, waiting to welcome me to my new life.

I'd never been to Norfolk before, and suddenly, I was living there. I travelled up from Essex that morning, leaving the home where my husband and I had planned to raise our children. I left a job in a school where I had taught since I left teaching college, to work at a small Primary-school in the village I'd only seen named on the application.

'Hevingham.' Who named a village that? It was the Anglo-Saxons of course, but it just sounded odd to an Essex girl like me. I may as well of been moving to Australia.

Why did a young woman move here on her own you might ask? The answer was simple. I couldn't stay, knowing that my husband was not coming back. Most of our early marriage was ruined by this thing that happened in the 1940s. It was called the Second World War, I'm sure you will all have heard of that.

On the day our troops finally won the war, tragedy hit me. I had just stepped out of the door to join everyone celebrating in the streets, when I was met by one of my former pupils. He was a telegram boy, and, in his hand, he held a note which I did not even need to read.

Aged just twenty-five, I was widowed.

For a year I struggled on alone in the place where we had planned to spend our lives. Everyone and everything reminded me of what was lost. Not all, but many other women in the village got their husbands and partners back and went on with their lives. Not me though, and by Christmas of 1945, I knew I could not stay there anymore, and I opted to move on for a new life.

It was two weeks before the start of the autumn term in 1946 that I moved to Norfolk. I spent the day travelling on the steam train from Essex to Norfolk. On the train, I kept myself to myself. I sat well away from the other passengers. I read the paper, ate my breakfast, drank tea, and smoked cigarettes. I kept my face hidden and didn't speak to anyone. I don't why because I'm very friendly.

The nearest train station was in the neighbouring village of Buxton, but I got a taxi from Norwich station to take me to my new home.

The village was deep into the Norfolk countryside and was split into upper and lower parts. My quaint little cottage was in the upper village, also know as the heath, a good mile from the school where I was to work.

After fetching a bucket of water from the well, I made a cup of tea— Yes, running water had not yet made it to that part of the village. I sat in the chair reading a letter from the headmaster of the school, welcoming me to the village and inviting me to meet with him that evening.

It was the sudden screech of the whistle from the kettle boiling on the gas stove that caused me to stand up and kick the table, spilling matches everywhere.

I hadn't even noticed the picture which had been placed on the letter to hold it down.

It was only when I sat back down in the armchair with my cup of tea and picked up the matches to light up a cigarette that I noticed something. The matches that had fallen from the packet were pointing in an arrow shape towards the centre of the table. It was almost like somebody had arranged them like that. As though they wanted to draw attention to the thing the arrow was pointing at.

It was the photograph of a young girl. It was nicely mounted in a gold-painted wooden frame. Once loved, it was now a little worn and scratched, but it was the picture, not the frame that intrigued me. From the limited knowledge I had of historical clothing I would say it was Edwardian.

At the time of writing, Edwardian times were over one hundred years ago, but back then it was not so long ago, so I would say it was forty years old.

It was black and white as all photographs were back then. There seemed to be something wrong with the child. It was as though her head was a little misshapen. Her eyes though, they felt as though she was peering through the glass at me, as if… No, surely the matches pointing in an arrow were a coincidence. A photo could not make things move.

I wondered if she lived here once in this sweet little cottage. She must be older now, far older than me. I was twenty-six—if I haven't said that already. I could not take my eyes off hers the whole time I sat smoking and drinking my tea. Even when I put her back down on the table, I could not stop looking at her. I walked out of the door backwards, still looking at her.

A frosty welcome

In his letter, the headmaster Mr Robinson had told me a few things —before anyone says it was creepy that he had a key to my house, the cottage was the property of the school, making me a tenant for as long as I was in the job. He told me that there was a bicycle in the shed at the back of the house. If I didn't want to ride, there was a convenient public footpath running behind the house which led directly across the fields to the back of the school. I did like a good walk, but for speed, I used the bicycle.

The cottage was in the upper village but the school in the main village. Despite being a smoker (Which they told us was good for us back then) I really enjoyed the fresh air and exercise I got from the bike ride.

I was going to love this place. However, after my first encounter with a local person, my mind changed a little when I entered the village shop to buy supplies.

'So, you'll be the new schoolteacher,' said the woman at the counter, grunting in an accent that I barely understood. This would be the accent I would have to get used to if I was going to fit into this place.

'Do I stand out that badly?' I smiled, awkwardly trying to make light of things.

'That you do gull,' she replied very slowly. 'Not just them posh teacher clothes, but that funny way what you speak. Oi can tell you hint from round ere gull.' (I can tell you aren't from around here girl)

'Judith Johnston, it's nice to meet you.' I smiled. My own accent must have thrown her. My accent was strange, because I'm a common Essex girl who blagged her way into teacher training.

The lady looked down at me as though she was not going to talk, but thankfully she had second thoughts. 'Elisabeth Bunn,' she told me, taking my hand in a loose grip. 'Wife to Roger.'

'Well, Mrs Bunn,' I smiled. 'It's a pleasure to meet you. Do you have any children at the school?'

Mrs Bunn shook her head, and sadly sighed. 'My boys are grown and gone the way of so many others their age.'

'The war took so many.' I breathed, feeling her loss as I ran my fingers through my hair. 'My husband and brother were lost there too.'

'Well, I'm sorry to hear of your loss.' She replied with a sad, solemn glare. 'I am sorry if oi misled ya. My boys have gone the way many of them do, but not to war. There's little work here for the young. The two boys of mine found work in the city.'

'Well, it's been great meeting you too, but I must be off.' I smiled, trying not to show my weakness as this misunderstanding brought back all the emotions I'd been trying to hide. As I tried to turn away, Mrs Bunn took my arm and pulled me back.

'If ya don't mind me asking, how long do you intend to stay?' She asked in earnest.

'W-well' I stuttered, slightly alarmed that she had pulled me back and somewhat unsure how to answer it. 'I-I... well, I suppose I never thought it through. To follow god's path for me if that means I'm to stay here for the rest of my life, I guess this is where I shall stay.'

'My guess is you haven't met the headmaster yet then?' She asked with a dark smirk on her face that made me uneasy.

In those days, things were not so formal in a job like teaching. With me coming from further afield, I was given the job without a face-to face interview due to my record.

When I informed Mrs Bunn that I was due to meet the headteacher, Mr Robinson that afternoon, she let go of my arm and shrugged. 'Well, that's your life, but I won't be surprised if after you meet him you get straight back in a cab and go back wherever tis you're from.'

'Well,' I sniffed nervously. 'I doubt I shall find Mr Robinson that undesirable,' I told her, turning to leave once more.

As I got to the door of the shop, Mrs Bunn called out to me. 'Oi guess they never told you why them other four teachers left then?'

I spun around on the spot. 'Other teachers?'

I stopped and listened as Mrs Bunn informed me of the fates of the four previous women to work in the post I'd come to take up.

The school had been two separate operations, but there was a power struggle and the head of the lower school for years, a Miss May, had been forced out by the current head, Mr Robinson. This move upset many of the locals. According to Mrs Bunn, the school had been on strike, and there was a protest which ran through the main street of the village, even making it into the local press.

However, it was all to no avail and since Miss May's departure only two years ago, no less than three more local teachers had been employed in the position, only to leave. All three rather quickly and for different reasons. 'Rumour has it,' she said grimly. 'That Mr Robinson's hands and eyes like to wander a bit.'

To which I replied, 'Well if that is the case and his hands do wander, he will find himself missing a few fingers.'

'Good woman,' she smiled. 'But be warned...' She continued in a darker tone. 'Some folk are comin' around to outsiders comin' to the village, and you'll find them a friendly bunch. Others... Well, they still hark back to the days when we hulled stuns at foreigners like yourself if they put a foot wrong, or even if they didn't.'

'Well thank you for the warning.'

'Any time,' she smiled, 'And good luck Miss Johnston.'

The headmaster

The school itself, built in 1875 was a typical victorian school building with a high sloping roof and large front window. It was surrounded by a hard play area, which would graze many knees. Even in modern if you look closely you can still see evidence that it was once two schools. There still is to this day an Iron gate for each school at opposite ends of the playground wall. There's also evidence of another wall that once split the playgrounds for the upper and lower school.

Another thing that's long gone is the headmaster's bungalow. It was right next door to the school grounds. There were two ways to the front door. One was a pathway, which led through a gate directly into the school playground. Today if you were to look over the wall, you can see the modern brickwork where the gate once was. The school gates were locked so I took the other path at the side of the house. I had to squeeze past a car parked in a small driveway, and from there, another path led through the garden joining the first one near the door.

The garden was a rainbow of roses and other flowers. In fact, there were so many bushes of different varieties that I almost didn't see an older man kneeling on the path as he tended to them. He nearly jumped out of his skin before standing up straight.

'Hello, I'm the newl teacher, Mrs Johnston.' I announced in a tone that suggested I was more confident than I was. 'I'm here to see the headmaster, Mr Robinson.'

'I do know what the headmasters called,' he replied with a grunt, shaking my hand.

I slapped my hand against my forehead. 'Of course, you do. You work for him.' I grinned stupidly.

'Best you come in then gull,' he grunted, showing me towards the door.

Inside the bungalow was just as nice as the outside. By that, I meant it seemed very homely and lived in. It was not dirty, yet not perfectly clean either, being someone who had lived on my own for some time now, I got a feel from this place that the headmaster also lived alone. Despite this there was photograph on the wall of young woman and baby who must have been his wife and child.

It was clean and tidy, yet it had a lived-in feel without a woman's touch. For example, there was a pile of dry washing in a basket by the door. For some reason, you could just tell it was done by a man. Dirty dishes left in the sink was another man thing. I just assumed that somebody in the position of headmaster, somebody who could afford a gardener, would have a wife.

The gardener showed me through to the small living room where there were a couple of small armchairs. The room was dark without windows and smelt strongly of pipe smoke. The old gentleman gardener nodded towards one of their chairs, suggesting that I sat while he made us some tea.

When he came back to the room, he sat in the other chair. 'So, Mrs Johnston.' He smiled pleasantly, 'How are you finding the village so far?'

I shrugged and explained that I had not been there long enough to get to meet anyone apart from the shopkeeper's wife. 'She told me some quite shocking things about the headmaster,' I explained.

'Oh,' he smiled, teasing. 'She loves to tell about how the headmaster has wandering eyes and hands. Does that sound familiar?'

'Very familiar...' I smiled awkwardly. 'But you work for him. Would you say he's like that? Because I'm sort of nervous about meeting him.'

I almost burst out laughing, when he replied, 'Well, I never caught the old bugger looking at me.'

'All the same,' I said, tapping my fingers gently on the arm of the chair. 'It sounds a little worrying to me as a woman who is going to be working with him. I'm just worried that Mr Robinson sounds like a bit of a womaniser. How long have you worked as his gardener Mr...'? I hit my hand against my forehead. 'Sorry, I forgot to ask your name.'

He laughed out loud, 'Mr Robinson.'

Well, that was embarrassing, thinking that my new boss was his gardener. Luckily he thought it was hilarious. It turned out that Mrs Bunn's harsh words about him were down to years of ill-feeling between the two of them. There were two sides to every story and about twenty-five years ago, when they were both single, she had tried it on with him, but he had turned her down, so she had been spreading nonsense ever since.

I did have to admit that I had been expecting Mr Robinson to be a serious well-dressed man in his late thirties to early forties, with a wife and children. Yet, here he was, a single man in his, I would say, late fifties to early sixties, who swapped a shirt and tie for gardening clothes.

It was a very informal meeting, and it was more of a friendly chat than anything. Mr Robinson just wanted to get to know me, and for me to get to know him. He knew about my circumstances, and he wanted to make completely sure that my head was in the right place, what with losing my husband and moving on to a new place with new people.

So, it turned out he'd been there and done that himself twenty-seven year early after leaving army at the close of the first world war. The poor man had gone off to fight in the war leaving his wife and daughter. He made it through the battle of the Somme, among others who didn't make it. Then, he spent time in a prisoner-of-war camp, and it was there that he received the horrifying news that his wife and daughter had been killed by bombs.

'My advice to you, girl...' he coughed. '...is take as long as you need to mourn but move on before it eats away at you like it did me.'

'I have no plans to remarry,' I told him bluntly, to which he replied that he hoped my attitude would change in time.

'Plenty of young fellas out there need a tough, stable, intelligent woman like yourself.' He smiled.

Changing the subject, I asked him about something that was nagging me. The answer I got saddened me at the time, but I didn't know how much it would affect my future. The question I asked was why three other teachers who took the job in the last couple of years had left so quickly.

'Well, between you and me, he smiled. The rumours that I'm hard to work with are a cover story for why those three women left the job.'

The first teacher to leave, Miss Kidd, had been forced out of the school by the governors, but Mr Robinson was used as a scapegoat for her departure, despite being very fond of her personally.

'Don't you lesten to Elisabeth Bunn' He scoffed when I told him what she'd said' Three more had gone since. The next teacher got herself pregnant out of wedlock and had to leave the post, but rumours of an argument were started by Mr Robinson to protect her secret. Another was from a neighbouring village and left to join her local school for easier travel. It was the fate of the last teacher that worried me somewhat.

'Victoria Ashworth. Lovely young woman much like yourself.' Mr Robinson sighed sadly. 'A sad, sad situation. The poor girl went crazy. She had this photograph of a young girl, a strange thing it was. It turned out she was talking to it. She thought it was talking back to her.'

I shook my head in dismay. 'What happened to the poor woman?'

'She's in Thorpe Lunatic asylum.' (In todays terms he meant a mental health hospital)

'And what about the picture?' I questioned, suddenly remembering the weird goings on that had happened back at my new cottage. The matches were pointing themselves at the girl in the photograph.

My heart gave a sudden quiver as he replied, 'Well, last I saw it, was up at your cottage on the kitchen table.

I didn't know what to say. Was it appropriate to tell him about my own experience with the photograph? If I told him, would he put me in the mental asylum too?

Thankfully there was no time to mention it as there was a knock at the door. Mr Robinson came back a few moments later. With him was a middle-aged woman who he introduced as Mrs 'Meddler, the school secretary. Mrs 'Meddler informed us that the rest of the school staff had congregated for the staff meeting in the Jolly farmers pub and were waiting for us.

Not so Jolly farmers

So, my new colleagues were all nice people. Even with a small school, it took a few people to run the place. There was Mrs 'Meddler, the school secretary, Mrs Manson, the cook, and her teenage assistant, Joseph, who also helped out his father, John, who was the caretaker. There was also Mr Robinson's teaching assistant, Sarah, who was in her late teens.

I was told that I did have a teaching assistant already assigned and her name was Jennifer. According to Sarah she had called round for Jennifer to be informed that she had been in bed with a sickness bug for two days. That was a shame, because from what they told me she was very much liked by all of them.

If only the older locals were all as friendly as my new colleagues. Standing at the bar of the Jolly Farmers pub waiting to be served, I had to wait while the barman served every local that stepped up, before finally acknowledging that I was there.

When I jokingly asked if they treated all newcomers to the village that way, he just shrugged and grunted. A man at the bar smiled and informed me that in this village you had to live there for twenty years before they treated you as a local. Then, an older woman lying on the bar corrected him by adding that it was forty years.

'It's nothin' personal,' the barman grunted. '...but local jobs should go to local people and not some upstart from down London.'

'Well,' I replied sharply, 'Firstly, I ain't from London, and secondly, if there were a queue of local teachers waiting for the job, then one of them would have got it, but as it is you're stuck with me.'

The old woman smiled weakly. 'This place is cursed, and I'll wager a bet in a year you are not here.'

Many of the locals drinking in the pub spoke to me in a similar fashion. It would have been disheartening if not for Mr Robinson reminding me that these people were just a few of the older generation of the village, and they were not the parents of the children I would be teaching.

Still, I was a little tipsy and nervous by the time I cycled home, barely remembering the way to the cottage. I found myself cooking my dinner on the gas stove around 11 p.m., before going to bed a little groggy around midnight.

I suppose this the lead into where the story began. All day I had been busy or around new people and learning about the place. This bit at the end of the night should have been the bit when I crawled into bed and snuggled up to my husband to get some much-needed sleep. That would have been the case if I still *had* a husband, but this place was so quiet you could hear a pin drop.

There I was in my nightdress with my cocoa, just butting out my last cigarette before bed, when I saw her there on the kitchen table glaring at me out of her wooden frame. It was as though she was begging me not to leave her there. I didn't know what made me pick her up and take her to the bedroom. It just seemed that I would be a little lonely.

Remember, we didn't have TVs to keep us busy in those days and there was no radio or gramophone upstairs.

I was sure that many people knew how lonely it could get when you lived on your own. It was even lonelier when you'd been part of a couple, but now you were back on your own. I was used to my husband not being there, and for the last year, I had known he would not be coming back. Yet, now I was in a new place where he had never been, I missed him even more.

However, something told me he wouldn't have liked it here. He had never really been supportive of me working. He was one of those people that thought a man should work, and women should stay home with their children. Yet, deep down, he knew he was not marrying a housewife. He also knew that I would refuse to marry him if he didn't let me go through with my dream of being a teacher.

It had been a contentious issue in the early days, but he came to see things my way. I wore the trousers, and he knew it. We would have done what I wanted in the end, moved out to the country and raised the kids. I just did it a bit sooner than expected.

As the wind creaked around the house, it was almost as though I could hear his voice calling on the wind. 'Judith, Juuuddditth, what are you doing in this shithole.'

I wished I could argue with him and tell him this was a nice village, and although I 'd heard the locals were a tough crowd, I was looking forward to my time here. He would have disagreed and said I'd gone soft, moving up North. I would have retorted that Norfolk was in the east and we would have a moan at each other then he would just admit I was right.

For some reason being in a new place made it hit me all over again. I was trying to read Jules Verne's From the Earth to the Moon and wondering if man would ever get there. The wave of grief took over me so suddenly, I had put my book down and picked up a handkerchief from the dressing table to dry the tears which were now leaking from my brown eyes.

As I picked it up, the eyes of the photograph seemed to look at me knowingly as if the girl in the picture somehow knew the pain I was feeling. Suddenly something fell onto the bed. I stopped crying for a second to pick up whatever it was.

The object was a small wind-up music box. On the top of it, was a figure of a small child sat alone with her head in her hands. *What an odd thing*, I thought, as I wound the little handle to see which tune it would play for me. Remembering I was supposed to be upset, I placed it back on the table and went back to drying my eyes. But then the box sprung into life, and it played a tune I knew well, a haunting, sad and lonely song with an uplifting end. We sang it with the children at school to encourage them to play with each other and not leave anyone out. But right now, only the sad part of the tune fitted to my situation, and it made me cry harder as I sang along in my head.

'Poor Mary sits a-weeping, a-weeping, a weeping. Poor Mary sits a-weeping on this bright sunny day.'

'Just change the name to poor Judith' I teased myself. I gave up trying to read. Eventually, I pulled myself together, dried my eyes and blew my nose, then turned out the light to go to sleep. Before I put my head down on the pillow, I rewound the music box in the hope the haunting yet uplifting end to the tune would help me sleep. Maybe, just maybe, I would end up happy someday, but for now, more crying.

As I rolled over, I caught a glimpse of the photograph of the girl on the bedside table. I could somehow see her in the dark like she was looking at me. It was like she was watching me.

The farm by the lake

Suddenly I was dreaming. I was by a lake. It was a green lake, more of a large pond. There were a jetty and a small boat, 'The HMS Maria'.

I wanted to play in the boat, but daddy said it was dangerous. I was a good girl and didn't want to get on the bad side of my father's temper, so I just sat there and kept myself to myself as I played with my music box. I didn't speak like the other children, but mother sang me the song that went with it.

'Maria sits a-weeping, a-weeping, a-weeping. Maria sits a-weeping on the bright sunny day.'

The song was supposed to be about Mary, but my name was Maria, so I changed it to my name, because I was special. Everyone who knew me said I was special anyway.

But hang on, this was not a dream about my childhood. It couldn't be, because my name was Kathleen and now Judith, not Maria, and I grew up in Chelmsford. However, for the purposes of this dream, I was eleven-years-old and living on a farm in Norfolk.

There was something not right about me either. I was not like the other children. I wanted to be like the others, but they wouldn't let me play with them. My mother told me it was because I was different, but I didn't know what she meant by different. They let me go to school when I was smaller, and I had fun, but some of the other children's parents said I shouldn't be there, so they wouldn't let me go anymore.

I struggled with clever person things like reading, writing and speaking, but loved to draw. But I didn't understand things sometimes. That made me angry and I couldn't control my temper. Sometimes when I didn't understand things, I did bad girl stuff, like hitting out at people.

I heard a person referring to me as 'The village idiot'. I didn't know what idiot meant, but as there was only one of them and it was me, I guessed my mother was right about me being special.

In the song, Mary got a playmate, but no matter how I tried, I never got one. It didn't matter how long or loud I sang, because nobody could hear me so far from the village. How did you make a friend if they didn't let you go to school? People went to school so that they didn't end up being stupid. I might be stupid, but even I knew that the way for me to learn not to be stupid was to let me go to school.

My little brother could go because he didn't look like me or shake like I did. He had playmates like Mary, but if he brought them home, I had to go and play in my bedroom, or stay away in case I misbehaved.

On the other side of the lake was the farm building where we lived with Grandmother and Grandfather. They worked on the farm too. Grandfather loved me and played with me when he could when nobody was looking. Grandmother didn't pay much attention to me. She paid all sorts of attention to my little brother and the new baby, but she didn't talk to me much. She hated me and moaned if I disturbed them by shouting and even had me beaten up for being bad.

Mum and Dad did love me, and so did my little brother, Jay. He played with me when there was nobody else. That was why I sang the song about Mary and her finding a playmate, because I wanted one so badly. I stared over the lake singing the song over and over. I found it hard to think that this was not real. It was just dreaming. I was Judith, not Maria, I was twenty-six, not eleven. I didn't live here. I'd never been to this place. The music box stopped playing. I bent down from the wooden bench where I spent most days seated, then I picked it up and wound it.

Back in those days, it had a back on it with a little mirror to it. I liked to look in it and pretend the girl who waved back was my playmate. I waved at her, and she waved back, but my eyes widened in shock. That was not me in the mirror, it was that girl. The one in that black and white photograph, but she was alive and in colour. She waved and smiled, but her mouth opened without me opening mine, and she spoke.

'H-H-Hello P-P-Playmate J-J-Judith'

I screamed so loud I woke myself up. The music box was still playing, but it had slowed down to an eerie place, almost threatening and sending shivers up my spine, somehow, still unable to open my eyes as they seemed locked shut, the vision of the girl in the mirror still burned into my eyelids. I felt along the wall for the light switch. As I found it and pushed it down, I tripped and fell forwards onto the bed shaking. Finally, I managed to force my eyes open, only for me to open them face to face with the photograph as though she was looking into my eyes.

So that was definitely where we came in.

The horse and cart

That dream scared me half to death. So much, that I went downstairs and made myself another cup of tea and lit up another cigarette. I busied myself reading the paper for the second time, finally falling asleep sitting in the chair. I did not dream again that night, and to be honest when I woke up, I felt rather silly for being so frightened.

In truth, had the dream really been scary? Of course it wasn't, it was a dream about a little girl playing with a music box. The face of the girl in the photograph probably only came into my head because she was in my mind from having seen her face before I dropped off to sleep. The music came from the music box which had been playing in the real world while I was awake.

***

Sunday morning, I was late for church and had to sneak in at the back. It didn't really help that I didn't have the sense to ask where the church was. History told us that most churches are outside of the village because of the superstitious beliefs of the Tudors, who thought that the black death was caused by the houses being too close to the church. It still baffled me that they could not only have such a silly theory, but then they went on to move so many houses away from the church instead of moving the church.

Given that I was supposed to be introduced to the village at church that Sunday, it was not a good start to my time in Hevingham.

Not everyone in the village was a churchgoer. Some of them were sensible and did more entertaining things on the weekend. Still, you must remember in those days everything was closed on a Sunday. From those who were there, I got a polite, but not overly welcoming reception. Mr Robinson, who made the introductions was keen to reiterate that this was because of me being brought in from down south instead of employing a local.

I was not saying they were rude in any way. At least they were not as hard to please as the lot in the Jolly Farmers. Perhaps sceptical was a better way of putting it. Thankfully, the children who would be in my class were not as wary of me as their parents. I often found that children were much more welcoming.

The jobs of the days that followed included some personal errands on top of school duties. This included registering myself with the local bank and with the doctor's surgery (This was pre-NHS which did not begin until 1948). Both were in Aylsham, which was a few miles up the road. I was very grateful to Sarah for showing me around the town, and to Mr Robinson for driving us there.

So, I had two full weeks before term started, and in that time, I had to write out lesson plans for the children in my care. It was a juggling act because each year group needed to be taught at their own expected levels. This was fine at a big city school where year groups got their own classes with one teacher per class. There were forty children in the lower school, but the ages ranged from four and a half years to eight-years-old, so they ranged from learning through play to basics in English, Mathematics, science and geography.

***

On the second or third night, the dream had repeated. It was pretty much the same as the first time around only I knew what to expect and as it drew to an end, I wasn't scared or filled with dread this time. Nor was I scared the third and fourth times I dreamed it. I did, however, wonder if this repeated dream was something in my head, or if the girl in the photograph was trying to tell me something.

More than likely, just in my head. Why would a photograph of a girl be trying to tell me something? It was unlikely that she was a ghost, not that I believed in such things. For all I knew, the girl in the picture was still alive. I guessed that the photograph was about forty to fifty years old. So, in her fifties or sixties. Hardly old enough to be a ghost. So, it was just my mind making things up. This woman probably lived in the village.

So, the dreams were not scary after seeing them a few times. The picture, however, was a different matter. I swore as I lived, that it seemed to follow me around the house. I would get up and go out in the mornings, leaving the picture by my bedside and would come home to find it waiting for me on the kitchen table. Believing I was going mad, I began talking to the picture like it was a friend.

Wasn't that what she said in the dream. She was lonely and needed a playmate. Perhaps it was me who was lonely, and because I had nobody real, then it would do me good to spill all my feelings out to this photograph. She didn't argue with me on my points of view on stuff I read in the paper. She beat my husband on that score, because he used to always have the opposite opinion to myself just for the hell of it, I thought.

The first day of school couldn't come quick enough for me. You'd think I'd be nervous about starting a new job, but to be truthful, I was itching to get going with it. I was certainly looking forward to the teaching part anyway, and it was dealing with the parents that scared me. Getting to know my new class and their abilities was my priority.

I was sat on board a cart with two horses pulling us. My father was transporting hay for the animals on the farm. I could come along if I kept quiet and didn't get in the way or get off the cart or try to talk to anyone. I did not understand why it was that I was not allowed to talk to people or get off the cart, but I just did what my parents told me. I knew I was not clever enough to understand why I could not do these things.

It was a nice hot sunny day, and I wore a pretty pink dress. My brown hair swung down my sides in pigtails. I was playing with my music box, but my father got annoyed and made me stop.

We were outside the school when suddenly there was a problem with one of the horses. As my father got off the cart to sort out the horse, I looked over longingly at the school where I was never allowed to go. There were children in the playground. All of them were running around and having fun playing in the sunshine, and there was me up on the cart being told to stay out of sight. I saw my brother down there. I was so happy to see him that I lost myself and jumped down from the cart shouting to him. 'J-j-j, h-h-h-hey it's m-me, M-mMaria.'

My brother, however, just turned away, ignoring me, and when one of his friends asked, 'Who's that?' He looked around and shrugged. 'I've never seen her before in my life.'

His words hurt me, because at home he was a good brother, and played with me, but outside of the home, he pretended I didn't exist.

When we got moving, my father scolded me for getting off the wagon. I cried a little after my telling off, and he softened a bit. 'You know you can't be doing stuff like that,' he soothed,

'B-but w-why' I ranted, a feeling of burning anger arose inside me. 'W-why can't I go t-t-t to s-school and learn with the other chchildren?'

'B-b-because,' he replied, mocking my poor speaking skills, 'You're the v-v-village idiot and if you weren't you know, they don't let people like you go to to school. One, you're not right in the head, and two, you are fifteen, and you are too old to be at school.'

I cried all the way home, and as soon as we got to the gates of the farm, I grabbed my music box, jumped down from the cart and ran towards the trees where I hid from my father.

When I got far enough from home, I opened the music box and investigated the mirror.

It was her face that looked back at me, the one from the photograph, but she was older here than she had been when it was taken. She looked at me as though she knew me well and she smiled sadly. 'Hello, Judith, see what I had to put up with when I was here. See how I was treated. I just want to go to school with the other children,' she told me in a hushed voice before repeating it over and over. 'I want to go to school. I want to go to school. I want to go to school.'

Then, all a of a sudden, somebody appeared behind her in the mirror, and there was a blood-curdling scream as though somebody had hit her hard, and I woke up sweating once more.

Miss Spelling

I used some of the spare days before the start of term to go around the village and knock on the doors of some of my class to introduce myself to the children and parents. After nearly a week in the village, I was still to meet my new classroom assistant. It worried me that she was going to be one of these people who was not interested in the job and more interested in getting paid. Mr Robinson, however, assured me that Jennifer must be very ill, because she never took a day off, even as a pupil.

I was now into my second week in Hevingham and I was about to go out on my bike to explore the villages to the Northeast. I opened the door on my way out and almost crashed into a teenage girl who had seemingly been reaching for the knocker.

I grabbed her just before she fell backwards onto her bicycle, which was behind her on its stand. She grinned a little breathlessly, apologising. From the look of her, she was fourteen at a guess fifteen at most, slim, pretty, all the things I never was. She reached for my hand and shook it with an enthusiastic smile. 'I'm Miss Spelling… Jennifer.'

Still in shock at bumping into this girl, my mind was not right for some reason. I thought she was a madwoman who had heard I was a teacher and wanted some help.

'Well, it's a bit odd that you would cycle all this way up here to ask me how to spell Jennifer, But it's spelt J.E.N.N.I.F.E.R.'

It was her turn to look at me like I was mad.

'You are the new teacher, Judith Johnston, right?' She asked with an air of scepticism. I nodded 'Well, I'm...' she paused, then she burst out laughing.

'Misspelling Jennifer...' She took a deep breath and composed herself. 'Sorry, it might've been better if I said Jennifer Spelling, known to the children as Miss Spelling, your class assistant.

'Ahhhh Okay' I replied once I'd stopped laughing, 'I was expecting a Jenniffer Brooks are you not the daughter of PC Brooks.'

(To avoid any confusion I'll explain that PC Brooks was not exactly our village policeman. He worked at Aylsham police station but Hevingham was one of several villages under his jurisdiction. He just happened to live in Hevingham, and my new classroom assistant was his eldest daughter, or so I'd been led to believe)

'Tha's right,' She replied brightly, 'He's my father but.... He's not, He's married to my mother, he's the farther of my little twin brothers. You know what I mean?'

I nodded, in understanding before opening my rather large mouth before I could stop myself and asked before putting my head in my hands as the words escaped. To my surprise, The young lady took my rudeness in good gest seeing the look of embarrassment spread across my face and reiterated.

'Alf Brooks has been a great father to me and tha's all that matters. Understood?' I nodded.

'It's a rare and wonderful thing for a man with such a respectable position in the community taking on another man's daughter.' (unlike today it was frowned upon by many for a man to take on wife who already

At this she burst out laughing. When she composed herself with a deep breath. -'You lost me at respectable.' She looked up at me with laughter in her eyes. 'He's a great dad to me and me and his sons but a respectable member of the community?' She smirked all over her child-like face. 'Me and mother lived with me grandparents at the time. He thought I was me mother's little sister. Shoulda checked before he her.... ' She laughed holding her hands out pretending to be pregnant.

I didn't know how to react to this very odd and very open first meeting. One thing was for sure. Working with this one was going to be fun or challenging.

'Between you an me, my stepfather does do a good job of keeping this village and the others in order.' She wagged her finger at me. 'But mind you never tell'm I said that. He is very good at the inspection of the public houses.'

I flashed her a grin as she told me, 'Right now he'll be in the Fox, then the Barleycorn, Jolly farmers, Malt and hops, getting up the energy to cycle over to the Marsham arms you understand?'

'The local policeman and the local drunk.' I said trying not to laugh as she grinned back.

'Honestly yes, but who doesn't love a copper who looks the other way when it comes to closing time.' 'she told me with a mischievous look in her eyes. It's actually good police work, hanging around the pubs because tha's where the local crooks hang out.' She stopped briefly for breath then started to talk at a hundred miles an hour again. 'He can't even figure out who kept pushing drunks in Westgake pit when they come out of the Jolly farmer's pub in the dark.'

I tried not to laugh once more, I'd seen what the locals called Westgake pit. It was a large duck pond made from a gravel pit, which has sadly been replaced by the village green many years ago. It just sounded like harmless fun.

'How did he try to catch them?' I asked seriously.

'Well' she smirked, 'He went and stood up by the pit to try to catch them, and guess what happened?'

I knew where this was headed.

'Somebody pushed him in the pit?' I nodded confidently.

'Somebody pushed him in the …..Oh you got.' She finished disappointedly.

'I was young and fun once.' I assured her adding, 'Was it you by any chance?'

She looked at me like I was stupid.

'Not me' she laughed, ' I'm a dear little thing I can't push a big fat man in the water. I got them Medler boys to do it for me.'

She could have been referring to anyone as half of the village had the surname Medler.

'There's not been a real crime in this village for donkey's years. Though I heard something about a murder once, down by on the camping ground by the beck/stream. Long before I was born tho.' *I later found out that the camping field was not somewhere where visitors pitched tents. The camping field was the last remaining sign of the game of camping, a sport played in Norfolk a hundred years earlier, which was banned after people several players died of their injuries. Reportedly nine players died a match in the down of Diss.)*

Jenniffer nodded at my bicycle leaning up against the wall ready to go out. 'So where am I taking you to explore?'

Just like that, I had a new friend and bike-riding partner. Jenn, as she liked to be called, was keen to be out in the fresh air. Rather than sit inside and talk, we went out for some girly bonding and rode our bikes. The ride to Aylsham was a good distance for me and I gasped for breath trying to keep up. Jenn didn't think the ride was far enough and apologised for not being able to go further, because she was still suffering the effects of her sickness bug. To be fair to the young woman, despite being younger and considerably fitter than myself, she looked every bit like a person who had spent a week being sick.

Despite not being sixteen for a week or so, Jenn had been working as the classroom assistant for the last year. She knew every child in the class and their strengths and weaknesses, which she had written out for me very neatly. She had even made short-term plans in case I never showed up.

Apart from the obvious with us both loving children and working in the school, Jenn and I had many things in common. She like me didn't know her father. Her mother had brought her up single-handedly until she married when Jenn was aged ten. She had two half-siblings just like me, she had two little brothers who she adored. My half-siblings shared the same dad, but they were older than me.

We both liked to read factual books as well as fictional, both big fans of Jules Verne as well older classics. She showed me her bedroom in their little house on Westgate street. It was a mini library with a bed in it. How on somebody so young, in such a remote place collected so many books was a mystery to me.

With both of us being fascinated by history, she was very keen to show me the sight of the bishop of Norwich's former palace near the fox pub. Nothing is left but the old moat. I'd like to believe there might have been some truth to the old wives' tales, which claimed that King Henry the eighth stayed there on his way to visit Anne Boylen at her birthplace at Blickling hall. I didn't like to tell Jenn that although Anne Boylen was born in Norfolk, she met the king in London so it was very unlikely that he stayed in Hevingham.

Later we went to my cottage to chat more about plans for the upcoming term.

Jenn was the exact opposite of those people who were unsure about me being in the village. As a person who had come from another part of the country, she welcomed me with open arms, and told me how great she thought it was to have a more diverse selection of people. She sipped her tea and grinned saying 'I think you and me will be a great team'

Around the time the clock reached five o'clock, she told me she had to go because her mother would be expecting her home for dinner. I smiled and told her I wished I still had my mum to cook dinner for me. As she walked past the table, she spotted the picture of the girl, and she picked it up for a better view.

'Victoria left this here, didn't she?' She said, suddenly putting the photograph down on the table.

'Victoria?' I shrugged.

'Victoria Ashworth, your predecessor. She went mad claiming this picture was talking to her.'

'Of course! Mr Robinson did tell me she is in a mental hospital.' I felt awful for the poor lady, especially after the dreams I'd had and the incident with the matches. I thought I might be going as crazy as she was but I wasn't going to tell Jenn that.

'*Was* in the mental hospital.' She corrected. '*Was* in the mental hospital. She was my best friend.' I couldn't help but notice a tear in her eye. 'I cycled over there three or four times to see her. I thought she was getting better but when I went last time…' She ran her finger across her throat.

'Oh god, shit, I mean of gosh I'm sorry' I gasped instinctively putting an arm around the girl's shoulders.

'It's fine' She shrugged, 'She's in a better place. Just don't tell old man Robinson. He thinks she's not allowed visitors because I told him that. I think he knows deep down. He's a lovely kind old man, he liked her a lot. It'd break his heart to know she's gone.' She paused reminiscing briefly, reaching into her skirt pocket and taking out a folded white handkerchief. For the first time that day, I remembered she was just a sixteen-year-old girl who'd lost a good friend.

'You haven't had a stomach bug have you?' I soothed. She shook her head.

'I told mum and dad I was ill and they stayed away' The poor girl sobbed. 'Left food and drink out for me but I just been sat there cryin'. I couldn't tell no one and you don't either.'

'I understand,' I nodded, letting her know I agreed with her mature decision to keep the death from Mr Robinson and the rest of the village. There was no need to upset her former pupils either. 'Better for him to think she's still alive than to hurt him with the truth. Nobody will hear anything about this from me.'

'Well, I'd best be off,' she smiled weekly after mopping her eyes with the handkerchief, 'I've had such a lovely day meeting you.'

'You too,' I smiled, patting her on the back. 'Come and see me any time you want.'

I followed out of the door to see her off, lighting up a cigarette and watching my new friend cycle off into the distance and telling myself I should have gone with her.

Before those uncomfortable moments, Spending time with Jenn had brightened up my day. Now though, I was alone to cook and eat my tea. I put the wireless on for some comfort and left my tea cooking. I tried to read a book, but I couldn't concentrate. Spending the day with Jenn had reminded me of what it was like to have a friend, but now she was gone I was lonely once more, and there was a sad song playing on the wireless.

I thought again just for a moment about what my life would have been like now if things had been different. I looked over at the other armchair where Jenn's teacup still sat on the small table. I could almost see my husband sitting there, relaxing with his pipe and slippers by the fire. There were four chairs at the dinner table and four plates in the sink. The radio was playing a much happier tune as two small children, a girl and a boy danced to the beat.

It was so surreal it could not be real. My husband was dead, and we had no children. I wanted children, but he was never that keen on the idea. That had been one of the few things we had disagreed over, but I'd always had the feeling that I would get my way. At that moment, I felt happy and warm inside, but I knew deep down this was not real and could not last.

I felt a sudden shiver. When the song finished the children both knelt with their heads in their hands and began to chant a familiar haunting tune. 'Poor Mary sits a-weeping, a weeping, a-weeping. Poor Mary sits a-weeping on this bright sunny day.

When they should have got to the next verse where they ask why Mary is crying, they just repeated the first verse. I couldn't help being scared and shivered as they removed their hands and looked up at me. Both looked me straight in the eye. Their eyes glassy and terrifying, and I shivered in fear.

'Poor Judith sits a-weeping, a-weeping, a-weeping. Poor Judith sits a-weeping on this dark lonely night.'

They did not stop there, and I screamed as their skin began to peel from their faces, but they continued to sing. 'She's going to rot away here, away here, away here. She's going to rot away here in this nasty place.'

I looked over to my husband for help, but he lay slumped in the chair. He wore his army clothes. There was blood seeping from his chest and head. He had been shot twice. I screamed and rushed to him, but he vanished into thin air.

I turned back to the children, but they too, had stopped singing, and they were just bones and dust. The tune, however, continued with somebody humming it. I looked up and down to see where it was coming from sitting back in the chair. Then, everything went dark.

There was no light in the living room and no fire. The wireless had lost its frequency, and it was blaring out background noise. The light in the kitchen was on but flickered violently. Then another shiver went down my spine. I had thought the nightmare was over, but there it was once more. It was coming from the kitchen table. A voice sang loud and clear.

I gasped and pinched myself because I was sure now, I was no longer dreaming. I was not dreaming,' Yet that photograph's lips were moving, and she was singing.

'And now you've got a playmate, a playmate, a playmate, a playmate. And now you've got a playmate, and you're here to stay.'

Then she winked at me.

I shivered, and she said brightly. 'Don't worry, playmate Judith, it will be okay.'

It went silent for many minutes as I took in what'd just happened. I tried hard to catch my breath. I felt in my pocket and shakily took out a cigarette which I'd rolled earlier. I was reaching over to the cooker to light it. My shaking hands rattled the saucepan which contained my food as I moved it from the hob. I burned my hand just a little, and it was enough to make me yell out.

Bang bang bang bang went the front door. I froze. Maybe it was the neighbours come to check on me or complain about my screaming. I rushed to the door with the burning cigarette in my right hand while I quickly wiped myself over with my handkerchief in my left hand. I didn't get to the door because it flung open. 'Judith, you okay? I heard you scream.'

Then as my eyes adjusted, my heart raced with relief. Jenn stood there in the doorway with a somewhat embarrassed look on her face.

'I'm okay,' I breathed. 'Just burned my hand, that's all.'

She nodded. She was dripping wet. It was tipping down with rain. 'I lost my keys.' She shivered. 'I came back to see if I left them here.'

There was something about what she said that did not quite make sense. Had she not said that her mother would be angry if she wasn't home in time for tea. It was funny that, because if her tea was on the table, then the door would not have been locked, and she would not have thought to look for the key.

I immediately questioned her on this as she searched the chair where she had been sitting drinking tea. Even if she had left her keys in my house, she could've come back for them the next morning.

'Okay, 'She breathed as she stood up from looking under the chair. 'I was home alone because my mum and stepdad took my little brothers to Great Yarmouth on the train yesterday. I stayed to feed the dog and the pigs. Lucky, they live outside, I fed them, but I couldn't get in the house to feed myself.'

'And?' I raised my eyebrow, 'The reason you lied about your mother having tea on the table.'

She gave me a teeth-clenched look. 'Well, my parents have gone away this morning. Taken my little brothers on holiday to Great Yarmouth. I stayed here to keep the animals fed. See there isn't another policeman to cover the area. If locals knew, then they would probably rob the post office or something.'

'I see your point.' I nodded, spotting her keys on the table behind the photograph. I moved into position so that she couldn't see the small bunch of keys. 'But it's better to look in daylight, and I'll come and help you.'

Knowing what I knew now about how depressed the poor girl had been, I didn't want her going home alone. The other part of me was over the moon that she came back, because let's face it, I was terrified about what just happened. After what she said, there was no way I was going to tell her what I just saw. Instead, I instructed her to get her wet clothes off before she caught a cold and to get into my spare nightdress.

Luckily, I had enough vegetables in, so I added some more potatoes and carrots to the stew pot to make sure Jenn was well-fed.

I only had the double bed upstairs, so I offered it to my guest, but she was the one to say that it was big enough for both of us.

Strangely, it might seem weird, but just having company calmed me and made me put the vision I had to the back of my mind. Sleeping in a bed with a young woman I only met that morning, seemed a good remedy for my fears.

The next morning, I confessed over breakfast, to putting the keys in my pocket when I found them. Jenn smiled and thanked me for making her stay over as she hadn't wanted to go home to an empty house by herself.

Despite the age gap, Jenn and I got on so well that we spent most days that week together at the school, planning lessons and sorting through all the equipment and supplies. Then, after feeding her family's animals, she came back to mine for the night. She didn't want to be sleeping alone in an empty house any more than I did.

There wasn't much to do in the way of entertainment in those days but when Jenn and I weren't at the school feeding her parent's animals, we spent the days discussing lesson plans or off on bike rides around the place.

A few times we were visited by Mr Robinson and or one of the other staff from the school. A very frequent visitor to the house was Joe, who worked in the kitchen. It was very clear he had a crush on Jenn, but she played it down. She made me laugh by regularly pretending she had a cold. However, when he told her he had tickets for the cinema and if she wasn't well he was going to take Suzy (Another girl in the village) Jenn suddenly recovered from her cold enough to cycle with him to Aylsham cinema.

The whole time she was there, I heard and saw nothing from the photograph or the phantom visions of children.

Unfortunately, on the Saturday before term started, she returned to her family, I was alone once again, and the visions returned.

Thomas and his friend

I hear so many teachers these days moaning and saying they can't wait for the weekend or the holidays. I was different. I supposed it was because I had nobody at home to make it worthwhile being there. I hated the holidays and weekends when I couldn't be at school, and to be honest, I hated going home alone in the evening.

I spent the night before my first day struggling back and forth from the well with buckets of water. Every pot and kettle I owned were on the stove, with a large pot of water boiling over the open fire. All this water once heated was poured into a tin bath meant for a child, which I could barely fit in with my knees up to my chest. Youngsters these days will never know what a chore it was to have a bath if you didn't have running water and a boiler and all the mod cons.

My only company as I sat there in the tub was that girl. Sat there on the table staring out of her frame. I wondered if she would laugh at my clumsiness, first when I slipped on my bottom and nearly tipped the tub over, and again when I tipped water over my hair and forgot to put my cigarette down first.

I would swear every time I did something clumsy, she smiled behind that frame of hers. It was almost like her expression was trying to change. That night I dreamed of her; I was her again. Something made me pick up the photograph and put it in my bag on the way out to school that morning. I took it out and put it on my desk, not knowing why I did that. But I supposed in some way I was doing what she asked in the dream.

,Despite it being on my desk that first Monday morning with all focus being on school and executing my lesson plans, I put the photograph and the dream to the back of my mind. School started at nine o'clock, but in those days the first bell was still rung at eight-thirty as it had been to get the children ready for school in the days when people didn't have clocks at home. Although with the size of the village, that meant those living two miles from the school couldn't hear it.

The first week was rather relaxed. I got to know the children in my class and their abilities. I was teaching the infant class and we taught four to eight-and-a-half-year-olds, so different-aged children had to do different activities.

The youngest got to play with building blocks and play dress up in the Wendy house, while the six to eight-year-olds learnt maths and English, and in the afternoon, we did Physical education, and then I read to them. That was not all we did at school, but you get the gist of it because we have all been to Primary-school at some point in our lives and you know what I mean.

It was morning break, and it was Jenn's turn to stand out in the playground with the children. When the kettle was hot, I made her a cup of tea and took it out to her, planning to go back inside for a quick smoke with the others in the staff room. However, when I got out there, Jenn took me by the arm and told me in a hushed voice, 'Judith, you need to see this for yourself.'

She took me to a secluded corner of the playground. It was at the back of the toilet block situated on the far side of the rear playground behind the main school building. These toilets would be remembered by generations of children in years to come for being a creepy falling-down building. You could look through the cracks on the wooden wall and see rusty chains swing. However, in those days flushing toilets were yet to make it to the school. The victorian out building contained wooden seats with a hole in the middle. The 1990s this horrible building was demolished and replaced with a garden.

Enough nostalgia and back to the story. What Jenn showed me was a child, a young boy in my class. His name was Thomas Smith. He was on the hard concrete out of sight of the other children playing with wooden bricks.

Thomas was six, but I'd already noticed that he had fallen behind the other children his age. Maybe this had not been picked up on because of the high turnover of teachers, but I'd already identified that he needed extra help with his reading, writing speech and mathematics.

It wasn't unusual for a child to want to play on their own, but we always encouraged them to join in with others. I was about to go to him and encourage him to come out and play 'Stuck in the Mud' with the other children when Jenn grabbed me. 'No just watch and listen to him.'

We stood back and observed Thomas for a while. He was playing with the blocks on his own, but he was talking to somebody else. Neither of us could see another child there. Without the pair of us being seen, we couldn't exactly go around the corner to look, but we listened.

He was asking the other child questions. He spoke very slowly, and he had trouble forming his words. This was something that I'd picked up on with Thomas, and his lack of speech ability might well have been his reason for avoiding playing with other children. He asked the other child questions about where they came from and what they were doing at the school. It seemed as though he was looking up at the other child and making perfect eye contact as they spoke, just as though there was really somebody there. But although no voice answered his questions, he seemed to react as though he had heard an answer.

Finally, after listening for a few minutes, I intervened. I knelt by him trying not to get mud on my long skirt and spoke with him gently. 'Tommy, sweetheart, who were you talking to just now?'

He nearly jumped out of his skin as though he had not seen me coming. He looked to me and then to the spot he had been focussing on then back to me. 'There was a girl who wanted to play,' He told me with a smile spread across his face.

Jenn took one look at me and walked away briskly along the grass at the back of the toilet block to have a look for the child. 'Does she have a name?' I questioned softly. He smiled and told me that she did, but he couldn't say it. So, next I asked him if she was small like the children in our class or bigger like those from Mr Robinson's school.

'Em!' he replied eagerly.

'Tommy who's Em?.' I asked gently.

'Her name not em.' He told me slowly adding, 'I can't it start with a M'

'Okay' I nodded before asking, 'Is she young like you or old like me?'

'Big girl' he replied confidently.

'And did she have dark hair like me, or did she have blonde hair.'

' Her hair is like Cousin Alice.'

'His cousin Alice is in Mr Robinson's class, her hair's brown.' Jenn informed me as she returned from searching the other side of the toilets, shrugging her shoulders as if to say she had seen nothing there.

She bent on her knees to speak to Tommy put a hand on his shoulder smiling.

'This girl M is she slender like me of plump like…..' I glared at her as she looked in my direction.

It was just then that we heard the main bell which hung from the school roof starting to ring out. Jenn looked at me in dismay, realising that we'd been so caught up in what we were doing that she should have rung the handbell to end break time five minutes ago.

Lunch was served in two sittings, one for those who had cooked lunch and those who had packed lunch. Teachers rotated sittings so that one of us was always there to support the dinner ladies with controlling the children. At dinner, I got Jenn to point out Thomas's cousin to me so that I could ask her a few questions and find out what she knew about his behaviour.

I cornered Alice on the way out of the canteen and asked her to come to my classroom to chat with Jennifer and myself. She was surprisingly compliant for a girl of ten and a half and came straight away. We didn't tell her what we had witnessed, but she was quick to confess that she herself was worried about her cousin.

The three of us sat on chairs hidden away in the corner behind my desk to give us some privacy. 'He's had a rough life,' she told me, nervously playing with her blonde pigtails. 'I'm too young to remember, but my mum told me, Uncle Jerrold, Tommy's dad was called away before he was born. He was stuck in a horrible place where bad things happened to him.'

'What sort of place was that?'

'He won't talk about it to me until I'm old enough to understand, but it had something to do with the war.'

I nodded, 'So Thomas had a rough time because of what happened to his Father?'

Young Alice shook her head, 'His mum died giving birth to him, and he didn't get to meet his dad until last year when the war was over.'

I sat there with my mouth open in shock. No wonder the poor kid was a bit messed up, absent father and a dead mother. I never knew my father, but my mum had always been there.

'Jenn!' I exclaimed turning to her. 'You're the village gossip, why didn't you tell me this stuff.'

I immediately felt guilty because I turned to see Jenn sitting there looking even more surprised than me. So shocked in fact that tears ran down her face. There was an awkward moment where Alice and I simultaneously offered our handkerchiefs to poor Jenn. She looked from one to the other of us as if we were mad and took out her own handkerchief to dry her eyes.

'So, do you help look after Thomas,' I asked Alice, once Jenn had finally finished blowing her nose.

Alice shrugged. 'Sort of.' She smiled uneasily, 'I walk him to school for Uncle Jerrold because we go the same way and Uncle Jerrold has to work long hours on the farm.'

Arrangements like this were common in the countryside in those days. It was a quiet part of the world with very-little traffic or dangers. Unlike today when parents seemed to find it necessary to drive to the school gate, very few parents walked to school with their children. Older children were often relied on to look after their youngsters.

'He's a good boy, Tommy.' She smiled, 'But he's quiet, and he struggles to make friends. It's like he's scared of other boys and girls.'

'We know exactly what you mean sweetheart,' I told her gently. 'Thank you for telling us this.'

Not wanting to worry her, we let her go back to the other children. I then went to the office to see if Mr Robinson was there so I could inform him of Thomas's behaviour, while Jenn went out to keep an eye on him.

The Smith's farm

After my talk with Mr Robinson, we thought it best to monitor Thomas for the rest of the week before involving his father. We were more concerned about the fact that he was behind with his work than anything else. His behaviour, however, continued to give us concerns.

On the fifth Friday of the autumn term, we decided it would be best for me to go and speak to his dad, and come up with a plan to help him catch up with his learning and integrate him better with other pupils.

Usually, we would do these meetings with two of us, but Mr Robinson had to leave school early that day to see his doctor regarding a private medical issue. When I asked Jenn if she was available, she gave me that apologetic, 'I really want to help you but…' sort of look. Then, she went on to tell me excitedly that Joe was accompanying her to see Errol Flynn's new werewolf movie. Although Joe had a crush on her she had a massive crush on Errol Flynn, who was old enough to be her Farther. I was happy for them both, to be fair. I remembered being her age and the pure excitement of entering adulthood. Even if Jenn claimed she had no feelings for Joe.

So, it was alone and slightly nervous that I went to see the Smith family.

I had met Mr Smith briefly when I did my rounds meeting the children and parents before starting my job. I hadn't needed to go down to their farm, I had bumped into Thomas and his father in the village, and he seemed a nice-enough chap. I don't want to give away the name real name of the farm where they lived so I'll call it 'Green Lake Farm' It was on the other side of the lower village from my home on the heath. It was up quite a long lane which ran off Brick kiln Road.

It was around 6:30 in the evening, but as the clocks didn't turn back an hour for another week or so, it was not yet dark. Remember in 1946 we were still working on what was called double British Summer Time. This was done firstly to make the evenings longer for farm workers during the war, and so the UK was working in the same time zone as Europe.

Despite being light, there were clouds in the sky, and it was cold enough to look like I was smoking. Although it was cold, I had to dab my head with my handkerchief to clear the sweat from cycling as I pushed my bicycle up the dirt track to the farmhouse.

I wasn't nosey, so I didn't snout around, but the farm seemed, from first looks, to be a reasonable size. There were fenced-off fields with pigs and sheep either side of the lane and a small stream which ran into a deep green lake, with ducks swimming on it.

Like a lot of farms, the house might once have been grand, but seemed to have fallen upon harder times. It looked a bit run down, maybe due to the stresses of the war, which was fair enough, because keeping the farm functional and feeding the people of Norfolk was much more important than painting a house or barns. For anyone looking for it building has sadly been replaced with a more modern one on the sight.

As I stepped up to the front door, a thought crossed my mind that as it was a farm, the adults were probably out working in the fields or having dinner. That left little chance of my visit being welcome at this time. I would knock in hope, rather than expectation, that I hadn't had a wasted journey.

Rather than knock straight away though, I thought it might be prudent to have a quick glance around to see if I could spy anyone working outside. As I gazed over the fields and the lake, the barns and trees, some sort of familiarity came over me. I'd never been here before, but somehow, I had been here a thousand times. It couldn't be real, but here was the very farm that I saw in my dreams, where Maria sat by the lake weeping and playing her music box repeatedly, where she ran to the woods to hide from her father. This place was real, and it was heavenly, yet strangely eerie. 'Stop it' I thought to myself. It could have been any farm with a lake. A lot of the farms in the village had man-made lakes filled from the stream.

Some of them were used as duck traps to catch them for food in years gone by according to Jenn. Anyway, Maria's lake had small trees around it while these ones were taller and thicker.

Regardless of my dreams and what was going on in my head, I was here to do my job. So do my job I must.

I knocked twice, but there wasn't a sound to suggest I'd been heard. I thought I'd had a wasted trip and had just turned to walk away when a gentleman answered the door. He could have been in his fifties and wore a flat cap and sported a beard. He smiled as he looked me up and down. Without a word to me, he stepped out of the porch and called back inside to his family.

'Margret, Om off om afraid. Dare's perdy young mawther out eer. I think I died and she's an angel come to take me hum.' *(Margaret I'm off. I'm afraid there's a pretty young woman out here. I think I died and she's an angel, come to take me to* heaven)

I just about understood his Norfolk dialect, he was teasing his wife, and telling her he thought the pretty young woman at the door was an angel who had come to take him to heaven. With my cheeky sense of humour, I played along, teasingly looking around and behind me as if to look for the woman he was talking about.

'I'm sorry, Mr Smith, is it? I can't see the young woman you described. Unless you meant me, which if you did mean me, I suggest you investigate seeing a good optician.

'Come in, gull, oil be guess'n you'll be eer to see young Jerrold.' He offered me his hand in welcome.

'Mrs Johnston, Thomas's teacher,' I smiled, shaking his hand. 'If it's not a bad time I need to have a word with his father about some incidents that have happened at the school.' At this, he gave me a knowing look as if he knew already why I had come to speak with them.

'Thas for you, bore,' *(That's for you boy.)* he yelled into the house, smiling at me. 'Hawp you don't mind me teasing ya, gull, and good comes back boi the way.' *(Hope you don't mind me teasing you and good come back by the way)*

Mr Smith Junior then appeared in the doorway all wet as though he'd been having a bath. He was a tall thin man of my own age with a weather-beaten look on his face, His eyes almost obscured by his dark curly hair.

'Sorry, I was just washing, been mucking the pigs out most of the afternoon.' He spoke in broad Norfolk too. 'What do we owe the pleasure, Mrs Johnston?' He remembered to call me Mrs, so that was a good start.

I put on my best posh teacher accent in the hope of sounding professional.

'Mr Smith,' I said shaking his hand. 'Sorry if it's a bad time, but I needed to come and speak to you about some matters involving your son, Thomas.'

'Well I'd be surprised if my son was called something else.' He teased.

'Well, Thomas is really happy in your class, so whatever it is you need to talk about, you're welcome here any time.' he told me as he held the door, adding, 'We were just about to have dinner.'

'Well, I'll come back another time then,' I said, turning back towards the path.

He caught my shoulder, 'Don't be silly, gull. Take ya coat off. Ain't no point in you coming all the way out here only to go home. We have enough food to feed an extra mouth if you're hungry and you can tell us your concerns over dinner.'

So, being invited round for dinner was a shock, but it would be rude to refuse such a lovely offer, especially as I didn't have a great feast waiting for me at home. I did feel bad for taking their food because we were still on rations. (*Many people think rationing stopped when the war ended when in fact it was in 1954*)

I was made to feel so welcome in their home. I felt like I was an old friend and not Thomas's teacher who his father saw once for five minutes. We talked honestly about my concerns regarding Thomas's behaviour at school over the past few days.

Their family situation was different from what I was used to dealing with. In the wake of the war effort, more women were going to work. Family situations were changing for the better. However, many families in the city still worked on the basis that fathers went to work, and mothers stayed at home with their kids, and that would still be the case for many. Many women were left in dire situations when their husbands went to war and did not return.

Although it was not unheard of, it was much rarer to meet a young widowed father. What was clear, however, was that Mr Smith, or Jerrold as his name was, despite him always being too busy to collect his son from school, was a good dad.

He might have been busy at work as people were, but he and Thomas had the best father-son relationship I'd seen in years. Much better than the troubled at best relationship I had with my father.(Or lack of) He also took a much keener interest then I expected in how his son was doing at school, and he thanked me very much for bringing the situation to his attention.

We left most of the talking regarding Thomas until after he'd gone to bed. It was best not to let on to him how concerned we all were that he was not only behind in school but talking to somebody who wasn't there. We decided among us that it was best to keep an eye on the situation, and not go rushing straight to a doctor. Children who were struggling with circumstances and the loss of a parent often found it difficult to make friends. Maybe he had invented a playmate for himself.

As for him falling behind with his work, I offered to spend some time with Thomas on Saturday mornings. Jerrold offered to pay me for my time, but I waved him away. In fact, I found myself looking forward to having something to do on Saturdays other than cycling on my own. The company would be nice too as they were all lovely people.

It had gone 11 p.m. by the time I decided I should be making tracks. I wasn't too keen on the idea of cycling through lanes in the dark, but there was no other choice. Having said goodbye, I was pushing my bike down the dark track to the road with a cigarette in my mouth—I didn't smoke in the house because very unusually for the time, none of the Smiths were smokers—when there was a noise, and light from behind.

Mr Smith Junior pulled up alongside me in a truck, smiling. 'Don't be a daft gull, thas way too dark for you to be cycling back up there even if you had lights.' With that, he jumped out and wrestled my bike off me and put it in the truck.

I stubbed my cigarette out before getting in the truck. Once we got going, I swore he was driving slowly so that our conversation lasted longer. I didn't mind because I liked talking to him. However, when the conversation turned to how he lost his wife, I must admit, I struggled to keep hold of my emotions.

Because we didn't discuss stuff like this in front of Thomas at dinner, I hadn't told him that Jenn and I had spoken to Alice. It was hard hearing it from the man himself, and I must admit I failed in holding back my tears.

His wife Mary had been pregnant with Thomas when he went off to war, reluctantly, in 1940. She found out after he'd left, but there was no question that he was Thomas's father.

He was sent to fight in North Africa where he was captured and put in a prisoner of war camp. He remained a prisoner of war until 1945 when the war ended. He spent years in a horrible place, and they held his letters from him. He could not communicate with his wife or family.

Thomas had been without any parents for his first five years of life. Jerrold had come home from the horror of the war camps, only to come back to a dead wife, a struggling farm, and a four-year-old son who didn't know him from Adam.

'It makes my story seem easy in comparison,' I sighed.

'Everyone's life is different,' he soothed in reply. 'I have a son to be strong for, but you. You live up here on your own in a new place with no support. Your life is harder than mine now. I'm home.'

'You're not wrong.' I smiled, admitting, 'I'm so lonely at times I've started speaking to a photograph of a young girl I found when I moved in.'

'That's truly awful.' He choked in surprise. 'But at least you can tell her about having dinner with us tonight when you get in before you go to bed.'

'I probably will,' I laughed. 'I wasn't expecting to have such great company tonight.'

He replied softly, 'Neither were we, Mrs Johnston.'

'I'm Judith to you outside of school.'

'Well,' he said as we pulled up at my house, 'Judith, or Mrs Johnston, whichever it is, I look forward to you helping my son, and you're always welcome at the farm whenever you're lonely.'

I thanked him for his kind offer.

As I was climbing out of the truck, I had a sudden thought. I'd taken the photograph to school with me, and she'd been in my handbag the whole time. If she really had lived at Green Lake Farm where the Smiths lived, then maybe Jerrold knew her.

He was a really kind gentleman; he'd helped me with my bicycle and walked me to the door. It was at the door where I took the photograph out of my handbag and struck a match to show it to him in the light.

I saw his face in the light as he saw her. His mouth was a little open as though he was going to say something like he recognised her or something.

'She seems somewhat familiar, but I can't say where I saw that picture before.' He put a soothing hand on my arm. It was enough to be friendly, but nothing more, as he told me, 'If you're struggling or feeling low, remember you don't need to talk to a strange picture when you've got friends at our house.'

'The same applies to you.' I smiled, and we bid each other goodnight.

Or so I thought.

Moments after bidding him goodnight, I stepped inside my home, flicking on the light as I did. As the electric light flickered on in the darkness, it was clear to me that something was wrong. There was something on the floor in front of me, and it was only when the light settled that I saw it and let out a shriek of terror.

Jerrold must have heard me shriek as he was walking back to the truck, because he came running in to check on me, shouting, 'Judith, what is it?'

Unable to move due to fear, I pointed to the floor, and he jumped back in shock. All the kitchen cupboards were open, and the teacups and crockery all smashed over the floor. The basket of kindling which I used to light the fire had been taken from the living room, and the wood was now spread across the kitchen floor. The debris from the smashed china was not, however, all over the floor as though it had fallen from the cupboards.

Somebody, some vile, sick person had been in my home. They had broken these things and spread them on the floor so that they said a simple sentence.

KATHLEEN I AM WATCHING YOU.

The family photograph

An hour later, Jerrold was still with me. We searched the cottage but couldn't find anyone. I was badly shaken and in tears. I didn't have a phone in the house so Jerrold took me straight to the home of Police constable Brooks.

Everyone seemed to be related to everyone else in the village. PC Brooks was stepfather to my amazing class assistant, Jenn, who claimed he was the best stepfather in the world, but also, worryingly, the worst policeman in the world. He was also the father of her two little brothers John and Michael.

As I've said earlier PC Brooks was not our village policeman, but he lived in the village and covered the area. There wasn't a police house in Hevingham he didn't have a car or instant access to back-up. All he could do was use the phone box to call the station in Norwich.

After a quick check around the house again, it was clear that whoever did it wasn't there. PC Brooks gave me the usual questions. 'Do you have any clues who could have done this and why? Does anyone else have a key to the property? And do you know who Kathleen is?' Jerrold stayed with me as I sat in the living room, shaking with nerves, I smoked a cigarette and sipped whiskey. The only other person who had a key to the house was Mr Robinson, and he was hardly going to do something like this to me.

'Kathleen,' I explained, looking from one to the other, 'That's my real name.'

I told him how I never liked my real name and how for years everyone I knew called me Judith, or Judy, with it being my middle name. Apart from Mr Robinson and the school governors, the only people who knew my real name worked at the doctor's surgery, the bank or the post office. Why would any of those people want to do this to me?

There was no way to tell who it was or why. PC Brooks explained that I couldn't stay in the house that night. The kitchen was now a crime scene, and the scene of crime team from Norwich would have to photograph it all in the morning.

The only people in the village who I knew well enough to ask to stay at their houses, were Mr Robinson and Jenn. Mr Robinson must have been in bed for hours, and Jenn obviously lived with PC Brooks and he told me that they didn't have a spare room. Jenn's room was too small for me to sleep in and he had a suspicion that Joe might be in there with her. Jenn however denied this later.

The only obvious thing to do, was to stay with Jerrold as he was there and his family had a spare room, he insisted. Plus, there was the obvious point that PC Brooks made, that he was one of only a very small number of people in the village who couldn't possibly be the culprit.

So, that night, a little tipsy and tearful, and very terrified, I returned to the Smiths' home, where they very kindly put me up in the spare room for what was left of the night. The photograph of the girl was in my handbag. I took it out and put it on the bedside table as I did at home.

It felt like having her there made me feel a little safer. I didn't know why she made me feel safe when she seemed to be in my dreams every night. She was just a picture, and the dreams were all in my head. Yet, I could not stop thinking that the place she had shown me in the dream was the very house in which I was now staying as a guest.

It was more the fact that the lovely Smith family were there that made me feel safe. All sorts of questions were running through my mind regarding who could have done that to my home and why. Who was watching me? What did they want with me? Why were they watching me?

In the moment that my body relaxed enough to finally drop off, a sudden thought crossed my mind. What if the matches that moved to write words under the photograph a month ago were not a coincidence? What if Maria was the ghost of the girl in the picture?

Until now I'd just thought these things were a coincidence. I'd read stories about stuff like this happening, but I didn't believe in such rubbish because of there being no scientific proof. Mr Robinson liked a laugh, but he would never have done something so reckless or childish. If he didn't do it, nobody else had a key, so the only explanation of it was that the person did not need a key. The only person who did not need a key was a person who did not need physical things. A person who could walk through walls, but as I said, that was scientifically impossible.

'I am watching you.' What did that mean exactly and how? Nobody was watching me, nobody human anyway, because to watch me they would have to have been somewhere I could see them. Unless they were using some sort of telescope or binoculars or something, then there was the question of why? A widowed mid-twenties Primary school teacher in the middle of nowhere was hardly a threat to national security.

The only pair of eyes that'd been on me regularly were those of the girl in the picture. If she really did move those matches, then who was to say what she could do if it wasn't all in my head?

The sun was in the sky, and I was in a good mood, the best I thought I'd ever been in. It was our first-ever family photograph. It was the first time I was allowed to wear my best clothes. The rest of the family saved their best clothes for church on Sunday. I wasn't allowed to go to church, I had to stay home with my grumpy grandmother. Mother said I couldn't go to church, because God didn't like people like me, because I couldn't keep my mouth shut. Children should be seen, but not heard, and, in my case, preferably neither.

I didn't know why my family treated me how they did. I was just happy for this one day to be able to feel like the rest of them, even if it was for one day.

The photographer came to our farm, and I sat by the front door watching him as he set up his camera. I'd never seen such a thing as a camera. I'd seen photographs but never the device that took them. I wanted to know how it worked. It did not seem right to me that a person could be transferred onto a piece of card. I tried to go and talk to the man about the camera, but mother told me not to bother him. I did it anyway, though. He showed me how the camera worked, and I nodded my head but I could not understand it.

MARIA'S PHOTOGRAPH

The photographer was a nice man. I think he understood that I was not like everyone else and he didn't mind. He let me practice posing for the photograph. I thought he was practising but didn't realise he had taken a shot of me.

The rest of the family came out to line up for the family photograph — my mother and father, grandparents, my cousins and my little brother. With a big smile on my face, I went to join them, when somebody put their hand on my shoulder, and a voice said, 'Not you, child.

Nobody wants to see a photograph of you.'

It was my grandmother. She smiled awkwardly. Awkwardly, but not nastily. She repeated so everyone could hear her. 'We are paying this man good money, and nobody wants to see the village lunatic in a photograph.'

I looked at my mother, but she looked over at my grandmother and pretended she did not see me. My father looked like he was going to tell her off, but he was scared of her, and he also looked away. I called out to the others, but everyone looked away.

'See,' she smiled. 'Nobody wants you.'

I felt a pounding in my head, the skin around my eyes tightened, and they became wet.

Deep down, I knew that I understood these feelings because I was Judith. I was not Maria. Maria felt the emotions and the pain from this horrible act, but she could not compute in her mind. She couldn't see why they would all be treating her the way they did, but she knew it was wrong, and a rage burned in her soul.

As Judith, I could hold my emotions even at the worst of times, as Maria I was about to burst. She knew no limits or boundaries, and she could not stop herself.

All of a sudden it got too much. I turned to my grandmother and I jumped as high as I could, and with all my might I whacked her with my hand, then I whacked her again. I watched her until she fell to the ground screaming that she'd been attacked without reason. The rest of the family piled in but I escaped and ran across the field. I ran to my safe place by the lake, but it was not safe because they could see me. My heart pounded in my chest, but I could not stop because I thought my father would give me the beating of my life if he caught me.

I woke up. It should've been dark, but it wasn't. It was in the same room where I was staying at the Smiths' house. There was a girl in the room, the girl in the photograph. Maria.

Looking at her, she could have been a little older than I thought she was in the picture. Twelve or thirteen maybe.

She was face down on the bed still wearing her smart clothes, but they were ruined by dirt, grime, mud and blood. The poor child was crying so hard that the bed was shaking. Not just as a teacher who loved children, but as a fellow human being, I just wanted to put my arms around this girl and take her away from this toxic place. But when I reached out to touch her, she did not know I was there.

There was a bang on the stairs, she heard it and began to tremble in pure fear as it was followed by another menacing bang and then another. Somebody was coming up the stairs and doing it slowly, banging their foot with each step to build fear in her poor little heart. With each step closer, she shook and cried more and more. Finally, the door flung open, and her grandfather stood in the doorway with his belt in his hand.

He closed the door behind him with a threatening bang. Maria sat bolt upright; her tearful eyes filled with terror. She jumped back off the bed and fell to the floor, then curled into a ball and cowered against the wall.

'Maria, we going to play a game.' He said softly, reaching into his pocket for what I thought was another weapon to hit her with. Instead, he put down the belt and took out a large white handkerchief and waved in her direction as though he was surrendering. He beckoned her over to the bed, and she nervously agreed to sit with him.

He reached over and whispered something in her ear. 'You understand, my love.' He said with a wink.

'I t-think I un-s-stand.' She stuttered, 'Grandad hit I am loud, ouch.'

It was clear to me from the way Maria acted and spoke that she had some sort of unseen learning impairment. That was why I think he double-checked that she understood.

'Ready' He asked.

'Re-ady' she nodded.

Her Grandfather picked up the belt and brought it crashing down on the bed several feet away from Maria who sat with her mouth open screaming at the top of her voice and he brought it down on the bed again and again. I counted ten loud smacks onto the bed. Each time Maria screamed louder despite being totally fine.

When he finished hitting the bed, he turned towards the door and yelled. 'Now let that be a lesson to ya, you horrible child.'

Then he sat back down on the bed next to his granddaughter, and he put an arm around her. She sobbed into his shoulder, mumbling something about how sorry she was. He picked up his handkerchief and mopped her eyes as though she was not capable of doing it herself. He held the handkerchief to her nose and got her to blow as my mother did with me when I was two or three.

'I did not mean hurt… grama, granda.' She stuttered.

'Yes, you did,' he replied with a wry smile. 'I been married to that old battle-axe for thirty-five years. I love her, but you gave her what she deserved this afternoon, my gull, and good for you.'

'Love granda.' She grinned.

'We need to get you some new smart clothes.' He smiled. 'I spoke to that nice young man with the camera and it seems that something may well be able to be done..'

The look on her face was precious. I never saw a child's face change from disillusionment to utter elation so quickly.

The old man smiled as he popped out of the door and came back with a plate of food for Maria and put his finger to his lips.

'They told me not to bring your dinner up…' he whispered. 'Didn't say I couldn't bring mine up though. Might leave it here.' He placed the plate on the bed for Maria.

The scene changed. Maria was sat by the lake again, and the music box was playing once more, Poor Mary sits a-weeping. Maria was sitting calmly on the bench by the lake. She hummed the tune to herself happily sitting in the sun with a board and a piece of paper. Somebody had plaited her long brown hair for her, and she wore it proudly around her shoulders. She kept looking up at the lake, and then down at the paper.

I crept towards her to look at her efforts expecting to see a mess on the paper, but my mouth fell open in shock. She wasn't drawing the lake as I had assumed. On her paper was the most beautiful drawing I had ever seen. Because she had been looking at the lake, I thought she was drawing it. The picture, however, was an absolutely stunning sketch of the Eiffel Tower in Paris. She could only have seen it in pictures, and she didn't even have one in front of her. It was all from memory.

Just then somebody approached Maria from behind, and as I heard them, she turned and smiled up at them.

'H-hello, Ma,'

'What are you drawing, my love.' She smiled kindly.

'Big tower in France.'

'Well, it's fantastic,' she sighed. 'I only wish you'd let me sell your work. I could sell it for a lot of money, or at least pay for food and clothes seeing as you'll never be able to do a real job.

Maria looked horrified at the idea of selling her sketch to anyone. She picked it up and pulled it into her chest as though she was scared her mother would take it.

Although I couldn't see her mother's face, I could tell she seemed very strained. Maybe it was the pressure of being a farmer's wife added to by the fact she had come to realise her daughter would be reliant on her both financially and emotionally, maybe for the rest of her life.

Despite the tone of her voice, her mother who could only have been in her early thirties clearly cared deeply for her daughter. I'd seen the look of guilt on her face as the grandmother had tried to push Maria out of the family photograph.

'I had a nice man calling at the house, Maria.' Her Mother smiled, 'He works with Mr Fox, you remember the nice man with the camera who our family photograph.

I saw Maria's expression drop as she turned away from her mother frowning.

'I was na in it.' She spat angrily 'Nana hate's me. You all no like me.'

'Maria stop' her mother commanded bending down and taking her daughter by the shoulders forcing her to look at her. 'That's not why I came to see you.'

Maria seemed to calm but she struggled to look away her mother.

'Listen Maria.' her mother implored, 'Before your Nana got angry, when you were practising standing still in front of the camera Mr Fox thought you so beautiful he decided to press the camera.'

I couldn't help thinking to myself that he mother was right. Maria not have like other girls in a lot way but she was certainly pretty.

Maria's eyes widened in surprise and wonder as she saw that her mother had a package under her arm.

'Than you, Maa' she grinned snatching the package as her mother passed it to her. She unwrapped it and threw the paper onto the bench.

Looking over her shoulder, I saw the thing that I suspected I would see.

Brand new and shining in its frame, the photograph of Maria that I'd found in my home. The one that was on the bedside table in the room where I was staying. I was in her bedroom with her photograph.

Nightmares

PC Brooks arrived early the next morning to tell me that police photographers from Norwich would be with us in the late afternoon. I had told him not to worry Jenn about it, but being his nosey stepdaughter, she overheard him talking and followed him on her bike to find out what was going on.

The Smiths had a busy morning on the farm, so Jenn and I decided we might as well make a start together on Thomas's extra tutoring. Thomas was well-behaved, and we talked about his life at school, what sort of things he enjoyed and what he wanted to do more of. This was the best thing to do rather than start to rush him into extra schoolwork right away with no lesson plan. There was no mention of the girl who he had claimed to have played with. Clearly, his young life had been very hard, no mother and no father, then suddenly meeting his dad at the age of almost five and having to adjust.

Later Jenn came with me back to my house and waited with me while the police photographers took pictures of everything in the house. When they finally left, Jenn kindly stayed to help me clean up the mess. Once the house was cleared up, she reached into her shoulder bag she had with her, and she smiled, taking out two sets of crockery and two teacups. 'I am staying for as long as you want.' She grinned.

'That's kind and I do love having you here, but I don't want you thinking you have to look after—'

'AAAAAAAAAAAAAAAAAHHHHHHHHHHHHHHHHHHHH-

HEEEEEEEEEEEEEAAAAA!' she screeched suddenly at something over my shoulder, making me jump and spin around, my heart racing to see what the scream was about.

There was nothing there. I then jumped a second time as something touched me from behind. Thankfully it was just Jenn rubbing my shoulders in an attempted apology for scaring me. 'Just practising my scream for if and when something does happen.'

Jenn stayed with me a month before I sent her home, knowing there was danger and that I needed to learn to deal with my demons.

I really did enjoy having her there, she made me laugh a lot, but could be cruel in a funny way though, as well as just funny. Like when Joe cycled all the way up from the village to see her one Saturday. We were having breakfast in our dressing gowns when she saw him coming up the path and quickly roughed up her hair, then took out her hanky and answered the door with a croaky voice. She told him she was contagious, and was about to push him out of door, until he told her he was going to take Suzan Burton to the pictures in if she wasn't enough. Jenn then made a sudden miracle recovery. I thought deep down, though, she really liked him, and she would be better off spending time with him than me.

Things were going well now. Life was good and I was spending every Wednesday evening and Sunday morning, after church, down at Green Lake Farm giving extra lessons to Thomas. His progress with his work was going on well, but our concerns were that at school he was still finding it hard to interact with other children. He was still going off at lunchtime. Either Jenn or I or Sarah or even Mr Robinson, would find him somewhere playing on his own. Yet, each time he was caught, he was always looking over his shoulder and smiling as if there was somebody there.

The Smiths were like family to me now. One evening Jerrold invited me to spend the day with him and Tommy in Great Yarmouth the following weekend. Sadly, the summer season was already over, and the attractions such as the fairground were tucked up in bed for the winter. It was nice to feel that they wanted me, and my work with Tommy was appreciated. We made plans to come back the next summer when the fairgrounds and the beautiful scenic railway were running.

My dreams reduced a lot when Jenn stayed with me. I expected them to return when she went away, but they did not. Not right away at least.

That night when I returned from our day in Great Yarmouth, I dreamed of my husband for the first time in a long time. It was not one of those dreams where your loved one appeared wearing a halo and told you, 'I miss you! I love you! I can't wait to see you when you get here.' No, no, no, he was not happy, he was angry with me for something I'd done.

He didn't approve of me going out and having fun with other people. It started with him knocking at my front door like he was a visitor. He yelled in my face asking me if our marriage had ever meant anything to me. Before I could reply, he struck me on the shoulder, then I felt a gut-wrenching pain as his other fist hit me in the stomach. As I was falling onto the armchair, he reached out and grabbed me by the neck of my clothes and slapped my face until it bled before dropping me on the chair in tears.

When I finally got the courage to look up, all I saw was the picture on the table gazing at me, and her lips began to move. She spoke softly and said, 'He's gone now you're safe. I awoke in my bed face down, and I cried until the sun came up and made it light. Forgetting for a moment that I was out of the nightmare, I crawled over to the dressing table where I'd placed a mirror, and I picked up the cup of water I always took to bed with me and splashed it over my face, thinking that it would wash away any blood from my beating.

But there was no blood, because there was no beating. It was all a dream; my cuts and bruises were gone. I reached down and removed my nightdress, then pushed back my hair. There was a reason why I always let the top of my hair hang down the side even when it was tied up in a bun. Underneath the flap of hair on my right shoulder, I bore the scars of my last beating. If it was not covered by my hair, then I would wear a band or ribbon around it, so people thought it was a fashion statement.

Before the war started, he was a gentleman, but when he returned on leave after many years away before finally being sent to his death, my husband was no longer the man I liked to remember him being. I would never show these scars to anyone because they were a sign that I was weak.

On the table stood the picture of Maria. Next to it was my tobacco tin which had been full of cigarettes, which I had rolled the night before. The tin was tipped on its side, and the cigarettes spelt the word 'HELL.'

'It was Maria,' I breathed. 'It was hell.'

End of term

It was a deathly cold December evening. School had finished for the day and Jenn had nipped home with her little brothers, before returning to help put everything away for the Christmas holidays.

There was a knock at the classroom door. When I called the person to come, I was not surprised to see the headmaster. This was not a surprise because he was my superior, and he often popped in to check on all the staff.

I spoke to the headmaster every day, before and after school and in the staff room. Today was different though. Today when I looked at him, he seemed different. Older, the grey in his hair was whiter and much thinner. He looked very thin too, almost frail, I suppose.

'Mrs Johnston, may I have a word.'

'As long as you stop calling me Mrs Johnston when there are no children here.' I teased.

'Well, Judith,' he smiled. 'School protocol is that I need to do a half-yearly appraisal for each of the staff. To reconfirm what an amazing job you've done since you came here.'

'Okay,' I smiled, beaming with pride at his words. 'Just tell me the date and time and place, and I'll be there.'

He smiled back, 'Shall we say a dinner date my house one o'clock on the twenty-fifth of December.'

There was something about that date that made me think it was a weird choice to hold a meeting. *Why would that be?* I thought to myself. Of course, he wasn't inviting me for a meeting, he was asking me to spend Christmas Day with him.

I then felt awful because I had to say no. To my surprise he was the third person to ask me over for Christmas, and I'd already said yes to both Jenn and her family and the Smiths. I would be going to Jenn's family for lunch, and then, later on, I would make my way down to the Smiths for dinner at Green Lake Farm.

I felt terrible thinking that the headmaster had gone to the effort of inviting me only for me to turn him down. Especially now I realised that he was going to be alone on Christmas, when I—who was expecting to be alone—had two invites.

When I told him I already had plans, I expected him to be upset and down, but as proof of the lovely man he was, he grinned all over his face and told me. 'It's brilliant that you're making friends in the village. I couldn't be happier for you. I just didn't want you to be alone on Christmas.'

'Well,' I breathed awkwardly. 'I'm sure Jenn's family, or even the Smiths wouldn't mind you tagging along. You can't be alone on

Christmas either.'

He had a reminiscing look in his eye.

'I won't be alone,' he said, looking at the floor. 'My wife and daughter are always with me in my heart. I guess you're the same with your husband?'

I shrugged, remembering the dream about him. 'He's more likely with his parents than in my heart.'

He turned to leave the room, but as he got to the door, there was a twinkle in his eye, and he grinned. 'What does a day mean anyway. Let's just move it forward a day. Can I see you on the twenty-fourth, same time?'

'Of course, I'll be there.' I smiled, teasing, 'But, remember, it's not really Christmas with no King's speech to listen to.' 'Oh no, what shhhalll we do?' he laughed.

Moving on, a few days later on the twenty-fourth, I made my way down to the headmaster's cottage via the footpath across the fields behind Avenue farm.

Walking the distance always worked up more of an appetite than cycling the same distance. The walk took around twenty minutes at a reasonable pace, and fifteen when I was in a hurry. There was no hurry that day.

As I have said, I usually for some reason took Maria's photograph with me to school because I felt it was where she wanted to be. However, I didn't usually take her to other places. Today, though, I could see her looking at me. She had to come; I couldn't leave her there. My husband's photograph was looking at me too, but I was still mad at him for hitting me in my dream a few weeks ago. I put Maria in my handbag, and I left Edward, my husband, by my bed, facing down on the dressing table.

In more recent dreams I'd seen Maria sat in her room talking to the photograph as though it was a real person. She told it how sad she was when feeling down, but on good days she told it when she was happy. The face in the picture never moved, she stared blankly. Sometimes I watched as myself, other times I was Maria, but more and more I was now the photograph itself taking in her memories and gaining a life of my own.

Living so deep out in the countryside I had begun to find a new appreciation for nature. I could even appreciate the foul stink of Avenue farm, which was at times so bad that I had to hold my nose as I passed the back fields, which I'm told to this day still look like a swampy battleground. I loved to see how the trees and animals changed throughout the year. When I first walked the path, the oak trees, the elms, and the chestnut trees were all in bloom.

The crops in the surrounding fields were harvested long ago, and the pigs and cows from the farms nearer the village had been moved inside. The autumn then came, and the leaves dropped and rotted away like we all would one day. The bushes and trees were skeletons with ice on them. In the summer it'd been teeming with wildlife, but that day all I saw was a single rabbit and a small fish in the brook.

The headmaster's garden was much the same. In the summer it was full of roses, but now it looked like the bushes were thin skeletal twigs.

I banged hard on the door and got ready to smile and greet the headmaster with his Christmas present. I couldn't remember exactly what it was that I got him, but it was alcoholic. There was a big grin on his face when he opened the door. He seemed younger than he did when I had seen him in the pub for our end of term drinks a few days ago. There was a spring in his step, as though just my presence in the house excited him. I knew how hard it was living alone, and any visitor to the house made me glad. |Even if it was the neighbour coming to tell me off for playing the gramophone too loudly.

When I stepped into the kitchen, it was clear he had gone all out for Christmas. There was food for more than the two of us.

Christmas dinner in those days was not like it has been for the past half-century. Turkey back then was a rarity nobody could afford, and the ingredients for what was now a traditional Christmas cake were just not around.

Dinner was rabbit with parsley and celery stuffing, potato cakes and bread sauce. The starter was carrot soup, and afters was carrot cake. No traditional Christmas cake or pudding, or mince pies. These things have become more common in the years since. There was one tradition we had back then, though that was already a long-standing one which is still around today in some form. A large decorated tree in the living room, a real living tree with candles, not one of today's cheap shitty ones. He even had crackers at the table.

I noticed as he showed me through to the lounge that there were three places set at the table. 'Who else is coming?' I smiled, looking around for them, thinking Jenn or Sarah was going to jump out at me.

'I invited an old friend.' He grinned, 'I think you will know this person.

I was puzzled. Who on earth of the headmaster's old friends would I know unless it was somebody from the village?

There was no time to ask as somebody grabbed me from behind and shouted. 'Guess who darlin?'

Jumping out of my skin, I freed myself from her grip and spun around. A woman stood there, she was slim and was in her early fifties, her hair had once been black like mine, but now it was almost all grey. We were nothing alike as people, but in looks she was just an older grey me. My eyes widened, and I threw my arms around and cried out.

'What on earth are you doing here, mother?'

A family Christmas

So, now things were awkward. It was lovely to see my mother. I did miss her at times, but how did Mr Robinson know how to find her? Was it true that she was an old friend?

From the way the two of them spoke to each other at dinner, I could tell that they went way back. Unless they had just got in touch and she had been staying in the spare room, and they'd got to know each other. Thankfully, it was clear that they weren't more than friends. The thought of my mother and my boss at it was. I won't go there.

Despite this, it was special seeing her there.

I loved my mum despite what I said at times. She might not have been bright, and she might have been very good at opening her legs for men, but I was far from the angry teenager I once was. I could see now that my mother was doing what she could to look after hungry kids. If that meant sleeping with people to put a roof over our heads and food in our mouths, then that was what she had to do.

It was lovely. We were all getting on so well. I loved my mother in small doses, and we had the sort of relationship where I could be honest and tell my mum that I could only deal with her in small doses and get a cheeky reply such as, 'The feeling's mutual.' Or 'It's me that keeps you at arm's length because you make me look stupid with all those brains in your head.' To which I would reply, 'I must be my father's daughter.'

We would always laugh and smile during these exchanges. Mr Robinson smiled across the table as he watched my mother and I get on so well. It was decided I should stay the night on the sofa so that I didn't have to walk back in the dark.

By late evening we lit candles around the tree and sat by the fire drinking from bottles of Stewart and Patterson beer. (A piece of local history. Brewed in Norwich from 1794 Stewart and Patterson bottles were lemon-shaped and stored on their sides rather than upright. Sadly they went out of business in 1971 after 197 years in business)

Around six o'clock Mr Robinson put another log on the fire, then went to the cupboard and brought out a large bottle of whisky. He filled three glasses rather generously, then he sat back in the chair and lit his pipe and smiled at us both.

I took out some cigarettes which I had rolled that morning and passed one to my mum, so we all relaxed in a cloud of what we did not know back then were cancer-inducing fumes. My mother looked over at the headmaster and smiled.

'I think it's about time we told Kathleen or Judith the truth before we all pass out drunk.' She smiled.

'About how it is that you two know each other?' I beamed.

'That and more.' Mr Robinson groaned. It was only as he smoked his pipe that I became aware of his cough. Maybe the smoke made it worse, I didn't know, but it was bad, and it sounded rough.

'Your mother and I go back to before you were born...' he sighed. 'I know, or knew, your father too, more's the pity.'

'You told me my father died in the war,' I said calmly, knowing she must have a reason for hiding this.

'You know men with families didn't get called up,' she told me bluntly. 'You ain't stupid, and you know I've been lying to you all these years.'

'I also know that baby does get born two years after their father died either mum. It's basic science mum.' I told her frowning. ' And by the way, Mr Robinson got called up, and he had a wife and daughter.' I pointed out bluntly.

'I was a career soldier in the army before...' he sighed. 'Rules were different for those of us already in the army and those who volunteered.'

My mother looked me in the eye. 'My husband was a banker in London. He never went to war. He was fighting the battle at home.' 'What happened to him?' I asked softly.

'Air raid,' she shrugged. 'He didn't get out fast enough, and he left me alone with kids to feed, and I tried to move on and find love again once the first war was over. I met a young soldier just back from the war, and he swept me off my feet.'

She looked at Mr Robinson, and I couldn't believe what I was hearing. I didn't know whether to be hurt or elated. Was Mr Robinson my long-lost father? Was that why I got the job at the school without an interview?

I asked him outright. 'Mr Robinson, are you my father?' But he shook his head telling me I've always been a good man and I've made many mistakes but I'm not your father.

'Your father was a horrible man.' My mother told me. 'He told me he loved me and your siblings, and we were engaged, but then when I got pregnant with you. He got cold feet and ran.'

'Bastard!' I shouted suddenly in anger. I jumped up and hugged my mother.

All those years I thought I was the accidental result of a slutty one-night stand until she finally told the truth.

'But where do you fit in with this, David, and how do you know my father?' I asked, confused, looking around at Mr Robinson and for once calling him by his first name.

He coughed for several minutes and cleared his throat before closing his eyes.

'I feel personally responsible.' He breathed, slowly and quietly.

'But why?' I shrugged.

'Because your dad was and is my youngest brother.'

My mouth dropped. 'You're my uncle.'

He nodded,

'But...' I was lost for words.

I couldn't think straight. I got up and left for some fresh air.

When I came back twenty minutes later, we talked calmly. Mr Robinson or Uncle Dave had been stuck in the middle, between loyalty to his brother and his blood family, and wanting to know and care for his niece me.

His brother—my father—was a nasty man who didn't want him to have any contact with my mother or me. Yet, the sweet, kind, amazing man, that I was now so proud to call my uncle, had been secretly sending money to my mother to help. However, he couldn't risk his brother finding out. After he left the army like many ex-high-ranking soldiers, he was selected for teacher training all paid for by the government to make up for the lack of teaching staff after the first world war.

All the time, he kept in touch with my mother. He was the mystery benefactor who paid for me to go to a teaching college all those years ago. When he heard from my mother that I'd lost my husband and was looking to move away, he made me the only candidate for the vacant teaching position here in Hevingham, so he could finally get to meet his niece and see what I had grown into.

'But why are you telling me this now?' I asked, helping myself to more whisky and lighting another cigarette.

He looked at the floor; then he slowly looked up at me.

'Because I wanted you to know your mother was not what you thought she was, and I wanted to get what I could of the family together for one last time.'

'What do you mean?' I asked. 'One last time? Why don't we meet up like this every Christmas? Why not summer too. Maybe the others will join us with their families.'

He shook his head. 'This will be the last time, I'm afraid. I'm leaving, and I won't be here this time next year.'

'You can't leave Hevingham' I protested, 'The children here love you.'

'As do I them, but the time is near.' He sighed and paused to cough into his handkerchief before continuing. 'I wrote a letter to the school governors, advising them that they should employ you as the new headteacher when I'm gone.'

'But you're not going anywhere.' I protested.

He looked me square in the eye, and said, 'I am afraid my doctor has a different opinion.' And with that, he showed me the streaks of blood on his handkerchief.

Cowboys and classrooms

Christmas day went by in an alcohol-fuelled daze. Both Jenn's family, who I visited for lunch, and the Smith's who I went to for dinner supplied me with beer and cheer.

The news that my whole life was a lie came as a shock. My dad was an asshole who used my mother and left her because he didn't want me. All this time I had an uncle who loved me, wanted me in his life, was giving me help all from far away. Now, just when I had the chance to know him, he was going to die. He assured me that there were a good few months left in him yet, but he knew. As he said that Christmas would be his last. A man who coughed up the amount of blood I saw on his handkerchief, did not last months.

I thought I laughed and smiled enough to show my appreciation for the love my new friends showed me. Despite this, I had a great time with both families who had taken me in for Christmas.

After Mr and Mrs Smith and Tommy were in bed, Jerrold told me to sit down on the sofa and have another drink, then to tell me what was wrong with me.

Finally, I told him everything I'd found out the previous day. I must have told him at a hundred miles an hour, but he listened as much as one who had consumed much alcohol could. I seemed to remember that once I finished telling him, I fell into his arms and burst into tears. The poor bloke must have been terrified.

I must've fallen asleep because the next thing I knew, strong arms were carrying me upstairs. I remembered mumbling something about how fit and strong he must be if he could carry my fat backside up the stairs. Then, it all went dark, and somebody whispered, 'Goodnight, Judith.'

I woke with a jolt and sat up in bed. The light was beaming through the windows and blinding me. It took a while for my eyes to settle. I looked around the room to get my bearings. It was the same room in which I went to sleep, but something was different. I stepped out of bed and walked towards the window.

The white walls were covered with drawings. They were not bad drawings like the ones that my five-year-old students did. The type that you told them were amazing so that they would take them home and put them on their bedroom walls. These were stunning examples of fine art. Maria's photograph sat on the bedside table where she often talked to the image of herself.

Suddenly the door opened, and a boy entered the room. Trying not to shock him, I put my hand up in apology in case I scared him, but then it was me that yelled out in shock, not him. He didn't see me at all, he just walked right through me as though I was a ghost myself.

I turned to see where he'd gone. My gaze found him on the other side of the bed. He was looking around for a moment. He must have been ten or eleven years old. His face seemed somewhat familiar, but I still was not sure where I'd seen him before. Maybe he was someone I knew, only younger, but how could that be if it was me that was invisible to him. He called out.

'I'm back. I fixed it. You better not be hiding again.'

I nearly jumped out of my skin again as the doors of a wardrobe, which I had not even noticed, burst open. A second person fell out of the wardrobe straight through me and onto the floor, probably hurting herself, but she seemed to bounce back up as if it was nothing, grinning all over her face.

It was Maria. She must have age three, maybe four years since the last vision that I saw of her in this room. She walked up to the boy very stiffly and tapped him on the shoulder, and said, 'BOO!'

The boy, who had obviously seen her coming was clearly playing along. He overreacted to her pretending to faint from the shock of seeing her. He seemed to play dead for a while. Maria looked worried and shook him as though she thought he actually fainted. She then clapped with delight as the boy jumped up to his feet like Lazarus on drugs.

The pair of them then sat on the bed, and she clapped her hands excitedly as he presented her with a wooden box. She opened the box, still unaware that I was looking over at her. She took out what looked to me like an earlier version of a toy that brought me much fun when I was a child. It was a 3D slide viewer.

Many years before the golden age of 3D movies in the fifties, there were these little viewing sets where you could look at any number of different 3D pictures which could transport you anywhere in the world. I spent many a day in my own childhood gazing at Paris, New York, and Rome.

'What do you say to me for fixing it?' The boy asked, almost in hope rather than in expectation of an answer, but she smiled. 'Th-thank you, b-brother Jay.'

She put the viewer up to her eye, and a big smile came across her face. 'While-west cowboy' She shouted delightfully. 'Bang, bang, you are dead, Jay.

She had obviously seen a cowboy from the wild west in the viewer. She put down the viewer on the bed and pointed both fingers at him shouting, 'Bang, bang, bang, bang.' The boy, Jay, rolled off the bed onto the floor hiding behind the wardrobe and shot back at her pretending to blow smoke from the barrel of his gun, before joining her back on the bed to look at more pictures.

It was clear from this to me that there was something very wrong with Maria, but I could not put my finger on what it was. They were just a brother and sister playing together like brothers and sisters did. I played wild west with my siblings all the time. Sometimes one would bring themselves down to the level of the other to help that person have fun.

Jenn was somebody who was excellent at getting down to the level of young children when needed. She could teach English to a very good level for a sixteen-year-old. She could be right at home joining in with five-year-olds playing dress up in the Wendy house, or rolling on the floor playing games. Then on a Friday night she would be drinking pints in the Jolly Farmers with the adults.

My point was that the Maria in this vision must have been around Jenn's age, more likely older, but it was her younger brother that was bringing himself down to her level and not the other way about. Obviously, she could speak and had a working brain, but there was something about her which was just hard to explain. here she was much older than she was in the photograph, but still very childlike. This I thought would explain why Maria had no friends or playmates, and why she was lonely and isolated on this farm. This was the reason she did not get to school.

Still, all this was just a dream, of course. Was it not for the fact that I had seen this farm in my dreams of her before coming here, I would have just thought of it as another strange dream? Still, I thought she was just something made up in my head from that photograph. My memory of the farm could have been wrong. It could be any farm really. There was probably no end of farms with lakes in North Norfolk.

I watched on as the pair of them continued to play. I was invisible, more of a ghost than they were to me. After a while, there came a call from downstairs, and the two of them looked at each other. Maria licked her lips at Jay grinning all over her face. 'Tea-time'

Jay got up and ran straight for the door, as most boys would. Maria, however, quietly picked up the photographs in the box, then she very deliberately put them with the viewer in a drawer in the bedside table. Then, suddenly, she looked right at me and said. 'I l-left them here for y-your p-playmate, J-Judith.'

A moment later I awoke in the bed with the cover over me. It was dark and cold, and I should have gone back to sleep. The dream and my curiosity now had me wide awake. I rolled over to the right of the bed. I felt my matches and a candle on the bedside table. I lay across the bed and reached into the Victorian bedside table, wondering what I might find. To my dismay, it was there. The 3D viewer. The very same one that the children had played with in the dream.

I looked inside, and immediately I saw the 3D cowboy which Maria had seen. I believed he was a genuine cowboy, not an actor. Many of these types of pictures were taken to document the days of the old west. This was a very faded black-and-white vision of a man herding cows. He had no gun, that was in Maria's overactive imagination. How many years it had been there, I did not know. Was it left there because she never grew out of her child-like state? Or was everything in this room left here in memory of a former occupant who never made it to adulthood?

I was a guest here. It was not mine to touch and it wasn't for me to go snooping around in search of ghosts. I had more pressing things to worry about.

Rolling over and dropping off to sleep again I soon found myself in a place that I Knew all too well. I was in a classroom at the school. My classroom but this wasn't my class. These children weren't familiar to me at all. The desk next to which the teacher stood was my desk only with far fewer marks on it. Across the top of the small blackboard. I saw the date neatly written in chalk. It read July 14th 1928 and under it were big letters were the words "Show and tell."

Seeing the date, if this was another one of the dreams about Maria, then time had moved on a lot. Surely she would be in her 30s now not at school.

'Mary' called the teacher, who was in her mid-twenties with dark hair much like my-self and with glasses. Her rather large rounded lower half showed that she was around a month away from giving birth. 'I'm sure you have something weird and wonderful to show us as always.'

A thin dark haired girl who was at a guess eight-years-old, in long white smocks made her way to the front of the class, having taken something from inside her desk. There was a little groan from a few of the small class. less than twelve. This and the teacher's tone of voice told me none of them were looking forward to hearing from her probably due to previous objects she'd brought to show.

'I found this in a cupboard in my bedroom.' She told the class proudly. 'I asked my mother and father who it was. Mother didn't know, father told me he knew and that her name was Maria but he wouldn't tell me anything else.'

Of course, it was the photograph of Maria. It was Twenty-years old almost Twenty-years-ago.

'So Mary could you tell us why exactly you brought her to see us today?' Asked the board-sounding teacher.

'Well,' The girl said thoughtfully. 'My father got upset and told me to get it out of the house because it made him uneasy. It looks like it moves sometimes.'

'Huuum' Said the teacher. 'Photographs can't move Mary. Is there anything else interesting about it? Where is she now?

The girl looked uneasy.

'My father only said something very horrible happened to her and wouldn't say what.' The girl shuddered, I think she died,' She paused, 'My father asked if Mr Robinson might want the photograph to teach his class about history.'

The teacher put her hand out to take the photograph from Mary. When she took it she looked at it with an expression of distaste.

'Eww, it does seem like it's moving. What an odd thing. ' Her hand seemed to shake as she passed it quickly to her young blonde assistant.

'I don't think It's old enough to use for history lessons Mary.' She looked at her young classroom assistant who must only have been about fourteen. 'I'm sure if Miss Spelling takes it to the headmaster he can make his own choice if he wants it or not.'

Mary went back to her seat and looked on as the class assistant took the photograph towards the door that led through to Mr Robinson's room. I noted the absence of the two big red wooden folding partition walls that were there in my time to divide the classrooms from the assembly hall. As the classroom assistant passed me unaware of my presence she looked up from the photo and I recognised her face. I should have known when I heard her surname. She was Miss Spelling just like Jenn, She was the spitting image of Jenn. Of course she was. It was Emily Spelling now known to everyone as Emilly Brooks Jenn's mother. More worrying was the fact that she was so young just years before Jenn herself was born.

In my shock at seeing her, the dream was cut short. As I awoke. In the drifting moments between sleep and the real world, I heard Maria's voice beside me whisper. 'Playmate Mary took me to school.'

MARIA'S PHOTOGRAPH

After my mother stayed a few days with the headmaster it was decided that I should go home with her and spend new years day down in Essex visiting old friends.

I enjoyed a few days playing catch-up with my sister Elsy and her children. But when it was time to go home, I was glad to be getting back. That was until my mother left it to the last minute to yell a vital piece of information at me through the train window.

In some ways I wish I hadn't heard what she said so then I would not know. She left it so late that she could not give details, but I got the gist of what she was shouting through the train window and why.

'Jenn Spelling is your cousin!'

My best friend and classroom assistant was my cousin. That could only mean that all along the headmaster had been Jenn's missing father. But if it was true why would he not tell her? Then I remembered my dream and how young Emily Spelling looked just two years before giving birth to Jenn and realised why I had to keep my mouth shut.

Back to school

The first morning back after Christmas break was cold, not as cold as it had been, but still cold enough to see your breath in the air. The road was icy, and I didn't want to chance falling off my bicycle, so I took the footpath across the fields. Many of the children who lived in the upper village also walked that way. It was almost calming to see the trees and fields white with frost. I often found walking to work was good for the soul. Of course, in those days very few people drove to work.

I remembered that walk specifically because it was one of the last few times that I felt calm and at peace. I was not aware that what was waiting for me at school would change the course of not only my day, but my life.

I arrived at school nearly thirty minutes later than I should have due to the torturous nature of the walk. I told myself that I should not be hard on any children who arrived late, because they were children, and as an adult, even I had struggled with the icy footpaths.

Jenn was there bright and early as normal, looking annoyingly smart, keen and ready for work. I didn't know how exactly I should talk to her now I knew secrets about her past, which she didn't know herself. If it was down to anyone to tell her the truth, it certainly wasn't me, but I didn't half feel bad for knowing.

So, it was a normal morning to start with. Jenn rang the bell to get the children in. I was halfway through the register when the classroom door opened. It was normal for a child or two to be running late, but this was not a child. It was Sarah, Mr Robinson's teaching assistant. She called Jenn aside and spoke quietly, and both waited until I'd finished calling the register before coming to speak to me.

'It's Mr Robinson,' Sarah told me in a panicked breath, whispered just quietly enough, so the children didn't hear. 'He's not showed up for work.'

'Well, he might just be running late,' I assured her, but she shrugged me off.

'I've been a pupil at this school since I was four. I've been his assistant for nearly four years. In all that time, he has never been late.' Jenn nodded in agreement, adding that he had never been late, not even once.

Before I could react, she was already on her way to the door, saying she was off to his house to check on him. I let her go, thinking she had the right idea, but as the door closed, I heard his words from the other night ringing in my head.

'The doctor says the cancer will kill me in months, maybe weeks.' I shot up and ran to the door faster than I had moved in years. Jenn was already halfway across the playground when I yelled at her to come back and look after the class. Fortunately, Jenn was a good girl, and did exactly what I told her without question, and Sarah went back to her class too.

Knowing what I knew, I could't let a sixteen-year-old girl walk into that house alone, knowing what she might find in there.

I went back into the school and got the next most senior person, the school secretary, Mrs 'Meddler. She came with me to Mr Robinson's house. We knocked on the door, and we called his name several times, but there was not a sound. Luckily in a village that had no crime, people didn't lock their doors, and we found Mr Robinson's door unlocked.

The kitchen of the bungalow was clean and tidy, and the living room was also clean, but stank of pipe smoke. Still, we called and still no answer. I would think I knew by now where this was headed.

I'd seen dead animals stiff with their souls removed. I'd been to more than one funeral too. But nothing, nothing could prepare you for the first time you saw the body of a dead human being.

He lay there, silent in his bed. Then from the mouths of myself and Mrs 'Meddler, escaped a breath as though we were both smoking, but from his came nothing. Only his face was above the bed covers, but it was twisted, and grey, and nothing moved. It only took the briefest of touches to know he was stone cold and stiff as a board and had obviously been dead for many hours.

Mrs 'Meddler, who had known him for many years, had already burst into tears. You would have thought I would be overcome with emotion too, and I was. Believe me I was shocked, and my heart was racing. I needed a cigarette, but a cold numb detachment came over me. I'd just lost my friend and mentor, and my uncle. I could have broken down, but the first thing that crossed my mind was the children. They don't deal with death easily. There were fifty young people over there in the school who needed me to be strong.

After a few moments of holding each other, Mrs "Meddler and I pulled the bed covers up over his face. We then made our way silently back up to the school. Jenn must have seen the look on our faces as we came through the door. She gave us an uneasy look and instructed the class to get out some of the play equipment before coming to speak to us.

I took Jenn to the side of the classroom, while Mrs 'Meddler made her way to the other classroom to speak with Sarah.

I never saw someone take bad news so well. I assumed she was in shock. Just like me as she didn't just burst into tears. She just smiled sadly and hugged me for what seemed an eternity until I realised, she had placed herself where she was so the children could not see her crying silently on my shoulder.

Jenn, being Jenn was not weeping long and was able to compose herself better than most, having discreetly mopped her eyes and whispered. 'Tell the class I've had to go home ill, and I'll go and get my dad out of…' She looked up at the clock where the little hand had almost reached the number ten, and she shrugged. 'Probably out of bed, but knowing him maybe the Jolly farmers.'

Goodbye Mr Robinson

Before I knew it, it was Friday and school was over, but I wasn't going anywhere. I was exhausted and full of cold. I'd hardly slept at all since that awful morning. I was putting a brave face on things for the children, trying to get the school back into working order after the loss of Mr Robinson. The bags under my eyes were almost as black as they were on the days that my husband beat me.

Looking back at the events of the week, it still seemed like a bad dream. We closed the school and put a backup plan into motion. We sent brothers and sisters home together, and those children who didn't have siblings at the school were put in groups that lived in the same area and sent home too.

PC Brooks sent for a doctor to call his death officially and for an undertaker to take the body.

We expected the children to go home and stay there, but that was not the case. In the time that he was alive, the headmaster never thought that he was liked. However, he couldn't have been more wrong.

As soon as news spread of his passing, what seemed like the whole village turned up at the gates of the school to see for themselves.

Soon, the playground was filled with parents, children and former pupils. All of them wanted to pay their own respects to their former headmaster.

There was an outpouring of grief like I had never seen. It happened in the most fitting of ways. Due to where the headmaster had parked his car, there was not enough space from the wall to take him down the driveway past the vehicle. This meant that the beginning of his final journey would take him through the gate which led through to the playground.

So big was the crowd that Jenn and I, with the other staff, had to help PC Brooks to clear a path in the crowd so that the undertaker could pass through. With no cameras to film the moment, events such as this were often lost in time, and only lived on in the memories of the few who were there to witness.

Everything was surreal like nothing I'd seen before in my life or would again. As the stretcher carrying Mr Robinson passed through the crowd, and the tears fell, they cheered and clapped him on his way. As he reached halfway across the playground, those gathered struck up a song to see him on his way.

It was his favourite hymn; one we often sang in assembly backed by Sarah's questionable piano-playing skills. This time there was no piano, just loud voices singing to him as he passed by. 'The Lord is my Shepherd.' Ironic that he loved to sing the song, but quietly admitted that he never believed in God.

Even in those days, physical contact with a pupil was frowned upon. However, it was safe to say now that Jenn, Sarah, and myself made it our duty to hug and embrace every child and parent, and any other person who had come to mourn. I was later told that my compassion on that awful day was what finally won me over with the locals who had not wanted me in the village.

When the last family finally departed and there was nobody left but the staff. Jenn went to the headmaster's cottage, then made her way back to the school. By now, there was a chill to the air once more, and the wind was whistling across the playground and rocking the trees.

We were clearing up the mess left by the children so that the caretaker didn't have to do it. You might ask exactly how much mess the children could have made in the short time they were in school that morning. Truth be told, there was no real need for cleaning to be done, but none of the staff seemed to want to leave. I thought that was because it would make his death seem more final. Life must go on, but with the headmaster gone, who knew whether things could ever go back to any sort of normal.

As none of us wanted to leave, all the staff sat for a while in the office, eating our packed lunches, drinking tea and smoking while we shared our memories of Mr Robinson. Despite what she had told me about no feelings for Joseph, Jenn spent the entire time we were in the office with her arm tightly around him as she cuddled into his shoulder.

I was last out of the office and I made sure all the cigarettes were out, before tipping the ashtray into the bin. I was shutting the door when I heard two shrilled screams. The first came from Sarah in the upper school. Before I could go running to see what had happened to Sarah, there was a second scream, this time from the direction of the lower school. Heart racing, I froze uncertainly, wondering which of my friends to help first. I made the quick decision to go to Jenn because she would not scream over something unless she was in trouble, while Sarah had probably just seen a spider or something.

I found Jenn stood in the doorway with her mouth open. She screamed a second time jumping out of her skin as I touched her lightly on the shoulder. As she turned and grabbed me for support, my mouth fell open. Everyone had been in the office, and the school had been empty, nobody had left, and none of us could possibly have done it.

The classroom was trashed, the old wooden Victorian desks and chairs were scattered around, and some were tipped over. In those days, we used ink wells in the desks to dip pens in for writing. Where the desks had tipped over, the wells had spilt onto the floor and in the dark blue liquid, something had been written that not even a daring and vile person would have said in those days. Yet in 2019 I felt I could say it without anyone batting an eyelid. It said in big letters,

'THE HEADMASTER F—ked CHILDREN'

Before I could open my mouth to gasp, Sarah came running into the room shouting and screaming for us to come and look. She shrieked even louder when she saw what we were staring at.

My classroom was not the only one trashed. Sarah led us to the upper school to show us the desks turned over in the same way and the same writing. It did not stop at the desks and the floor. Every blackboard was covered in chalk, and every piece of paper was scribbled on.

A meeting from hell

Just like when my home was ransacked, Pc Brooks had been summoned and so were the police photographers. However, nobody could be found, and nothing could be proved. The school was shut for both Tuesday and Wednesday while we cleared the place up and gave the children time to mourn their headmaster. That night Jenn had come with me, claiming she did not want to be on her own, when in fact she had a family at home to support her. I was pretty sure she came, because she wanted to look after me knowing I had nobody.

The school could not remain closed. So, we reopened on the Thursday, and it was a strange muddle. With one teacher down, I had to take over the upper school, while Jenn took over teaching the younger children, and Sarah flitted around between both classes helping where she could. Mrs "Meddler had contacted the education board and the school governors. However, the governors couldn't gather at such short notice, so it was the following Friday after school that I was to meet with them all for what would be the first time.

The children were brilliant, they didn't know everything that had gone on in the past few days, but the upper school couldn't have been better behaved. I was mentally and physically exhausted by the week's events and lack of sleep. Even when I did sleep, I would not only see visions of Maria, but now the beatings from my husband in my sleep were more frequent.

I was nervous about meeting the school governors. I hadn't met with them when I first joined the school due to it being such a rushed appointment. My hands shook at the thought of meeting them under these circumstances and trying to explain to them how I was doing my best not to muck up their school. I had no explanation for the damage that'd been caused by the desks being knocked across the floor, and we were no further towards finding out what happened. I was a lower schoolteacher with no upper school experience, trying to teach subjects which I hadn't studied since I was at college. What if they thought I was so bad that they just decided to close the school and hire two new teachers? A new head and one to replace me.

It was 3:25 p.m., the school had finished ten minutes before, and the rest of the staff and I were supposed to meet the governors at 3:30 p.m. I was sitting at the desk coughing, sneezing, and shaking with nerves as I rolled a cigarette. Maria's photograph was on my desk and for some reason so was the picture of my husband, although I could barely bring myself to look at it.

I was talking, but there was nobody in the room. I was talking to Maria asking her to wish me luck, knowing of course that I was going out of my mind talking to a photograph, just like poor old Victoria. If I was caught, I wouldn't be surprised if I was put in a mental hospital just like her.

Bang, bang, bang, went the classroom door. I jumped out of my skin.

'Who could it be?' I asked Maria almost expecting an answer. 'Staff don't knock on doors. it must be a parent. In that case I should not be having a conversation with an old photograph.'

'COME IN,' I called to the door at the far end of the room.

As the door opened, I hastily packed away my tobacco, dropping the tin on the floor and thankfully not spilling it. After bending down to grab it, I looked up to see my visitor. He was tall and handsome.

'Now, now, Judith, I hope you were not planning to smoke that cigarette outside of the designated area.' He grinned.

'Jerrold… I mean, Mr Smith.' I breathed, sitting back down in my chair with relief that it was a friendly face.

'How are you?' He smiled, with me grinning back at him.

He was welcome anytime. As I mentioned earlier, we had become very close over the weekends that I'd been going down to the farm to give Tommy his extra lessons. Plus, I also went out for day trips with them, and Christmas dinner. That sort of thing. Basically, we knew each other well. In fact, Tommy was already much improved and probably at the level he should have been for his age now.

Were it not for the fact I love spending time with the Smiths, and we still hadn't got down to the bottom of this girl he had told me about, lessons would have ceased?

I felt a sneeze coming on, so rather than reply, I took out my handkerchief and gave him one of those knowing looks that says. 'Just let me sneeze, and I will tell you all about it.'

I sneezed so hard I near fell out of my chair, and it was quickly followed by a second sneeze and a third. Finally, I stopped and managed to blow my nose before standing up.

'It's good to see you, but why did you knock when you don't need to, because you're you?' I smiled.

'Well, I heard you talking so I…' He paused, 'Who were you talking too?'

'Myself,' I lied with a laugh.' We were arguing as you do.'

'Stress of the situation,' he grinned uneasily. 'Sorry I haven't been around to help.'

'You don't have to be.' I smiled. 'Just because I eat the beef that comes from your farm, that does not make me obliged to help you out if the fence gets broken. So, in the same way, just because I teach your son, you don't have to come and help me when the school goes into meltdown.'

'True.' He smiled, 'But, as a friend, I want to help.'

'Do you have a gun on your farm.' I smiled playfully. He nodded. 'Can you go and get it?' I teased, 'Then you can shoot all the school governors, so I don't have to meet with them five minutes ago… *Oh, shit, I'm late!*' I yelled, quickly making my way to the door.

Jerrold followed me and we talked and walked at the same time. He was telling me not to panic and that the governors would not worry if I was a couple of minutes late.

'You don't know school governors,' I panicked.

Quickly poking my head into the office on the way past, I lit up a cigarette and took two or three huge puffs before stubbing it out. Then I stopped at the door and blew my nose again with my rather well-used hanky.

'You can't come in I'm afraid' I smiled, 'Sorry, whatever you came to see me about will have to wait.'

He nodded. 'I know you've got a lot on your plate right now, but is there any chance of you meeting me afterwards.' He smiled awkwardly, very kindly thrusting his clean handkerchief into my hand, so I didn't have to use my yucky one. 'If you're too tired, we can do it another time.'

I groaned, 'I'm exhausted. But if it's you, then it must be something important.'

'It's about who trashed the classrooms after the headmaster died.'

I nodded silently and smiled. How did he know about that? Nobody was told apart from the police so as not to scare people. Thomas would have said nothing, and Jenn hadn't told anyone, so how did he know?

'Okay,' I grinned, thrusting money into his hand. 'Meet me in the Jolly Farmers after the meeting. Get me an extra-large pint of whatever you're drinking and wish me luck.'

With that, I opened the door to face the governors.

Jenn, Sarah and Mrs "Meddler were already there, as were a few people in suits who were sitting around the table. One seat, however, was still empty.

So, many of the governors were people who owned businesses in the local area. I knew some of them by face, but not by name. For example, the chairman of the governors, Mr Thrower, was a local brick merchant who often passed me, going the other way in his cart as I cycled to school. Just a few short years later poor Mr thrower was driving his cart laden with bricks when it overturned in the lane behind the Barleycorn pub. He broke his neck and died at the scene. He was a lovely man who did a lot for the community.

Another, Mr Fox, owned a timber yard in the village, Mr Brewer, who was a farmer, and somebody I knew well, the local vicar and last, but not least. Mrs Peg, the upper school parent representative. There were also two men in suits who I had never seen before. They introduced themselves as Mr Price and Mr Pennyworth.

Both were from the Norfolk Board of Education.

The meeting began by everyone introducing themselves to those of us who did not know each other. It was usual to do this and break the ice a bit before getting down to business. The head of the governors, Mr Thrower, then began to recall to everyone the history of the great work that Mr Robinson had done at the school and how he would be sadly missed. Suddenly, there was a knock at the side door, then somebody entered the room.

It was Jerrold! I was about to curse him for intruding when to my shock and amazement Mr Thrower welcomed him in.

'Ladies and gentlemen, I'm sure you all know Jerrold, he's the new parent member of the board of governors.'

'Sorry I'm late, everyone,' he smiled. 'I had to go back and get my gun as Judith asked me to murder you all in cold blood, so she didn't get sacked.'

You could have heard a pin drop in the room, then, suddenly, the room burst into roaring laughter.

'I did only mean for him to shoot you all in nonvital places,' I grinned, looking around the table.

'Why didn't you tell me you were on the board of governors.' I hissed as he sat down in the spare seat next to me.

He laughed. 'I just wanted to see your face when you found out.'

So, there was a lot of the usual waffling that went on at these meetings. The governors asked me to tell them my side of what went on with the incident after the headmaster's death and how it was dealt with. However, they didn't seem too concerned about it in the grand scheme of things, but all agreed it was a horrible act of vandalism, and we shouldn't rest until the culprit was found. Jerrold, however, gave me that look that told me he still wanted to talk to me alone on the subject.

So, we moved on to the subject of the plans to get the school through the near future and the challenges we faced.

'Well, I hear young Jenn here has been doing a great job in the lower school.' Mr Thrower shot her a proud look. 'However, you are all aware that we can't have an unqualified sixteen-year-old teaching the class long term.'

'Well, we best get on with the job of finding a new headteacher so I can get back to my class.' I paused to sneeze, 'I miss them.'

The governors all looked at each other sheepishly as I wiped my nose.

Mr Thrower cleared his throat, 'Well, yes, we've already been talking about this subject in your absence.'

'You're already looking?' I breathed in a sigh of relief that I could soon be going back to the lower school.

'Well,' He told me calmly. 'We are looking for a person to replace you in the position of infant teacher '

A fit of burning anger coursed through me, 'What you're sacking me? Sacking me after all this?' I replied, standing up to walk out of the room in anger. However, Jerrold pulled me back with a calming arm around my waist as the rest of them stared, then looked at each other not knowing what to say.

'Judith, sit down. He's not sacking you.' Jerrold soothed.

'Well, good headteachers are very hard to come by.' Mr Thrower said to the room. 'Especially halfway through the school year, seeing as most of them are wanted where they already work. Then we have had so many reports from parents, especially Jerrold here, who has told us all about how you gave up your weekends to help his son.'

'Well, I love helping children learn. That's what makes me happy,' I smiled, adding, 'I don't mind doing it for free as well as my normal teaching. Plus,' I smiled at Jerrold. 'The Smiths are such an amazing family, and I love helping them.'

So, it turned out that they had all been at it. Everyone, all members of staff, apparently, and many of the parents had been asked their opinion over the last week and a half that I'd been running the school.

'I propose a vote,' Mr Thrower grinned, getting to his feet.

Jerrold raised his hand, 'I second it,' he beamed.

'What vote?' I asked, puzzled.

Mr Thrower ignored me and addressed the room. 'All in favour of recommending to the Board of Education that Judith Johnston is offered the position of headteacher of Hevingham Primary school, permanently.'

What were they doing? I was not old enough or mature enough, or even good enough to take on the role of the headteacher.

I stood there with my mouth open as hands went up around the room. Jenn's hand was first up, and there was a look of disappointment on her face when she was told as she was not a governor, she did not have a vote. The decision was unanimously in favour of offering me the job.

I was in shock. I didn't know how to react to the offer. I just sat there stunned in silence. I took a sip of tea and wiped my nose. You could hear a pin drop.

'What do you think, Judith?' The vicar asked.

'Well, not many people know that my real name is actually Kathleen.' I teased, 'But you offered the job to Judith so if you want me to do it, you'll have to have another vote.'

Just for laughs, they all raised their hands once more, but I sat quietly.

I looked down at the table, resting my chin in my hands, 'I don't want the job.' I breathed, to gasps around the room. 'I don't think I'm old enough. I don't think I'm mature enough, and I have no experience of teaching older children.'

The atmosphere in the room seemed to flatten with my words. Mr Thrower was about to speak, but I raised my hand to stop him without looking in his direction. The room seemed to hold its collective breath. I took my time and swallowed down the last dregs of my tea. I considered what I was going to say next.

'However,' I grinned, looking up at Jenn, Sarah, and Mrs "Meddler, then over to the governors and the men from the education board. 'If you all think I'm the best person for the job, then you must think it for a reason. So, I'll take the job…' I paused again, holding my hand up to

Jenn to stop her jumping to her feet in applause. 'On two conditions. One, I get to stay in my little house near the heath, because I love walking to school through the fields and don't want to live in the house and sleep in the bed where the headmaster passed away. And…' I looked at Jenn in particular, 'No celebrating because I only got this opportunity because a good friend has died.'

There were nodding heads around the room and murmurs of laughter when Jenn winked and told me that she wasn't going to cheer.

'I stood up because you were taking so long, I had to stand up because my legs are full of pins and needles.'

BANG…

Everyone jumped out of their skin, and the room was filled with panicked voices.

Every one of us had seen what just happened. The table around which we were all sat had just risen an inch off the ground and slammed itself back down to the floor, then lifted itself off the ground once more.

My heart was beating out of my chest, and my head was spinning. Jenn's eyes were bulging out of her head. Sarah looked like she was going to cry, while most of the men in the room just stared wide-eyed. The table just seemed to be floating in the air in front of us and floated for a clear three or four seconds before slamming down once more.

In their chairs shaking, the representatives from the education board looked at each other and started to collect their belongings as did the governors. Jenn and I exchanged frightened looks.

As we all exchanged terrified looks, a second noise made us all jump out of our skins once more. It was the click, click, click of Mrs "Meddler's typewriter, typing away as though nothing had just happened. I could understand if she was sat at her own table typing and not seen the main table lift off the floor, but when the table lifted, she had fled back to the edge of the room, tripping over her chair, and she was lying on the floor holding her leg, yet the keys of the typewriter, just like the table, were moving on their own. It finished with a 'Ping' when it reached the end of the line.

Standing up, my first thoughts were to check on Mrs "Meddler to make sure she wasn't badly hurt. Jenn was the first one to reach out and take the paper from the typewriter.

'Well,' she quivered. 'I guess the school ghost gives its approval.'

She passed me the paper from the typewriter. I read it out loud. 'Judith/Kathleen. Congratulations on your new job and good luck. Sorry for scaring you love Mar…' The last two letters were too faint to make out, but I was sure who it was. 'Maria'

BANG! The typewriter started again. The keys were flying furiously this time as though a crazy author was banging out a violent novel at breakneck speed. It stopped with a 'Ping' once more.

I took the second piece of paper, discarding the first.

It read ' Kathleen I'm still watching you and I'm furious with you. You dirty haw. I will have my revenge.' It went on to say some more horrifying personal things.

This second piece frightened me so much that I shoved it in my pocket, picked up my stuff and ran.

Hidden wounds

Jerrold and Jenn found me a good half an hour later. I was sitting in the Jolly Farmers at a table alone, where I was shaking so much that the embers from my cigarette were in danger of setting the place on fire. They set their drinks down on the table and pulled up two chairs next to me.

Jenn regularly drank in the Jolly Farmers despite her being sixteen and her stepfather being a policeman. When I had asked her if he knew, she had replied, 'Who do you think bought my first pint?' She paused adding, 'What a sixteenth birthday party that was. It weren't though, mine I was twelve.'

That was beside the point though. It wasn't just me that was seeing and hearing these strange things. Everyone in that room had seen it, Jenn was shaking like me as she brought the second pint of beer from the bar before sitting down.

'Thanks' for the drink Jenn.' I shivered.

She looked at me sideways with wide eyes, and gasped. 'These are both for me.'

She tipped the first mug back and finished it in a matter of seconds, then she picked up my tobacco and started rolling a cigarette. I was all for sharing and Jenn was quite welcome to share my tobacco if she didn't take it all, just that I'd never seen Jenn smoke before. In fact, she was the one who would put herself on playground duty, so she didn't have to go into the office while Sarah, the headmaster and I were smoking.

She took a deep drag. Her eyes widened, and she looked like she was going to be sick. She coughed violently, then with a look of disgust, passed the cigarette to me. In my shaken daze I took it from her and smoked both cigarettes at once.

'I thought those things were supposed to calm you down, not kill you,' she wheezed.

'Only if you're already addicted to them.' I breathed hard.

We were joined at the table by a few of those who had been in the meeting. Mr Thrower, Mrs "Meddler, Sarah and the vicar. Over at another table, I could see the men from the education board looking concerned at me, drinking their own beer rather quickly. This was concerning considering I believed they were driving the nine miles back to Norwich.

Mr Thrower cleared his throat. 'What happened at the school this evening does not leave this table, or we will all be in the madhouse.'

I didn't know how long we were in the pub, or how we managed to get away. I awoke in a warm soft place. My head throbbing, I was too exhausted to care and snuggled up to the warm person next to me.

In my sleep, I saw a vision of Maria with her brother out playing in the snow. 'Judith, come and play with us,' she called, 'You too, Jerrold and Thomas, and you Jenn.' We were joined by another young woman, but she never said her name. We spent all my dream throwing snowballs at each other. That was until I saw a person watching us from the track. He got closer and closer, and before anyone could stop him, he was upon us. He grabbed me around the throat, shouting and swearing. He swung back his fist as though he was about to hit me. I closed my eyes and waited for the crushing bruising punch.

I heard three crushing thuds, but no pain. His hands fell away. I opened my eyes. Jenn and Jerrold, and Mr Smith senior stood before me. All three of them had shovels in their hands, and my husband lay bleeding on the floor. Bleeding and as dead as he was in the real world.

Jerrold flung his arms around me, checking me all over to make sure I was okay, then he took me in his arms, and kissed me passionately, and my heart raced all aflutter.

I knew it wasn't real, but that was okay because when was I going to get the chance to kiss the real Jerrold? Wow—what a feeling it was.

I woke tightly snuggled into someone. I was still drunk from the night before and couldn't open my eyes with the early morning light hurting my head. Despite this, drunken me was enjoying the thought of kissing Jerrold, and decided that being drunk would be a good excuse to make a move on him. With my eyes closed, I moved slowly up to him and kissed his cheek and attempted to slide my tongue into his mouth, leaving no consideration for the fact that I had a cold and should not be kissing him. To my shock, but amazement, he did not push me away, and he started to kiss me back.

The more I kissed him, the more I thought something was not right. His face was smooth, his shoulders were not as broad as I thought, His arms seemed skinny, and he was long and…

'Oh my god…' I was kissing Jenn, and worst of all, she was kissing me back. I opened my eyes and pulled away quickly.

'Jenn I'm sorry, 'I breathed sharply, to which she replied sleepily. 'It's okay, it was nice.'

'What?' I said, a little louder making her jump.

'I mean, yuck, get off me you madwoman!' There was not much to convince me in her tone.

I could see her face in the early morning light that shone through a crack in the curtains. By the tone of the light, I guessed it must be around 9 a.m., but I might have been wrong. There was a weird flashing effect in the room, which suggested that although the sun was in the sky it was being blotted out by falling snow.

Jenn looked as though she found the situation quite funny, and there was a big smirk on her face.

'Why were you kissing me back?'

'You must have been dreaming,' she winked, but why was she winking? Was she thinking there was some sort of girl on girl thing happening between us? I mean, I loved Jenn as a friend, but I didn't want to kiss her, and I hoped she didn't want to kiss me. Seeing that I knew there was a possibility she was my cousin it was more complicated.

'Alright, I was dreaming about something horrible…' I confessed. '… but Jerrold saved me from it, and then he, well… kissed me.'

I looked up at our surroundings, but everything was blurry. We seemed to be sitting on a sofa—possibly at Jenn's parents' house.

'So, you want to kiss Jerrold,' she told me, sitting back on the sofa with a sceptical look on her face, stretching her arms.

'Well,' I shrugged. 'I did in the dream, because he saved me, but you know we're just friends.' I didn't add that she saved me too in case she wanted to kiss me again.

'I know no such thing,' she grinned. 'You and I are just friends, but that didn't stop you kissing me a moment ago.'

She winked at me again, as though she had thought I meant it.

Jenn moved back so that she was sitting on the arm off the old sofa, giving herself a height advantage over me. 'Well, it's a simple question, do you want to kiss him or not?'

'Well, a kiss is a kiss,' I frowned. 'It's not the whole package. That's much more complicated. You must consider that we can't have a relationship because we've both got pasts and what if it's not what he wants. We have to consider Thomas in all this, because he's at a stage where without his mother, he needs his father even more.'

'But you won't take his father away from him.' She smiled, 'I've seen you all out together, always three never two. He needs his dad to be happy, and you make his dad happy.'

'But I can't be in a relationship,' I told her quietly. 'There is so much that none of you know about me.'

'You think it would be an insult to your husband's memory?' I nodded in reply. 'Edward, that was his name, right?' I nodded again.

'Well, I think he would approve of Jerrold.' She grinned.

'You can't know that, you never met him,' I said coldly. It was only then that I became aware that I wasn't wearing the ribbon around my head. It must've fallen off, and I must've subconsciously touched the scar on my head. It was only then that I realised she'd seen it because she looked right at it and winced.

'Ouch, what happened there?' she exclaimed.

'I walked into a door many years ago.' I smiled awkwardly.

'My aunt did the same thing once.' She grimaced, 'My dad arrested the door, and it did a few months at His Majesty's pleasure.

'Good.' I smiled, pulling my hair over the scar. I straightened myself up and blew my nose into the hankie that Jerrold had lent me the night before. 'You won't tell Jerrold any of this will you?'

'I promise not to do anything bad.' She grinned, drawing a halo around her head with her finger.

'But that's just it though,' I teased. 'Telling him everything might be a good thing in your opinion.'

'I don't need to tell Jerrold anything because he already knows,' she smirked.

'But how on earth would he know?' I shrugged, raising my shoulders into an over-the-top expression.

Jenn looked down at the sofa as if she was trying to stop herself laughing at something.

'What's so funny?' I raised my eyebrows. 'How does he know what I said?'

Jenn pulled the most awkward twisted face I had ever seen anyone pull, then she looked at someone behind me.

'So, Jerrold,' she grinned nervously, as I spun around in shock to see him sat right close to me. 'I've never been to your house, and I need an excuse to get away. Can you tell me where the toilet is?'

He pointed over to the door. 'Hut out the back, Jenn, and don't use all the paper.'

He waited until Jenn was out of the room. I thought this was going to be the bit where he told me I was not welcome in his home anymore because I could never replace his lost wife.

But when I turned to look him in the eye, he smiled at me gently.

'I su-su-suppose that you heard everything I said just then?' I breathed, still fighting my thumping head.

'It was a private conversation.' He beamed. 'I only heard it if you want me to of heard it, if not it's forgotten.'

He took me by the shoulders so he could look me eye to eye, but he said nothing, then he smiled and pushed my hair back to look at my scar. Normally I wouldn't let people touch my face, but he was allowed within reason.

After a good look, he whispered gently. 'You should not need to hide that from people.' To which I nodded silently.

I looked down at the floor. 'I get fed up with the questions. Or those who stare and judge or judge without asking.'

He nodded slowly looking down where he found the ribbon, I'd tied around it was hanging loosely around my neck. Without asking, he took it and untied it. I thought he was going to hand it to me, but instead, he picked up my handbag and put it in the side pocket, then, without a word, he unbuttoned his shirt and threw it to the floor.

Although there was only a crack of broken light, it was enough for me to see the reason he had removed his shirt, was not so I could feel his abs.

I gasped in horror, and now I felt awful for worrying over a tiny scar on my head. Jerrold's chest and stomach were covered in long deep scars. It looked like he must have been hit with a horsewhip. I stopped there with my mouth open and shook my head.

'Bloody Germans' I breathed, but Jerrold shook his head.

'Everyone blames the Germans.'

'But Alice told me you were a prisoner of war?'

He shrugged, 'Alice is a child and a good one at that. She was told nothing, but must have overheard something, but she jumped to the wrong conclusions.'

'Children often do.' I agreed, 'But they didn't do this?'

He sighed and looked at me for a second, then what he said was something in touch with place and time, 'Let's say that it was something involving Japanese people.'

Who could blame him after what they'd done to him? The stories I'd heard from those horrible places. People assumed he was in Germany because most were. Those camps in Germany were terrible places like hell on earth, but the Japanese camps were something of far deeper evil.

'Tommy's never seen the scars,' he whispered. 'Neither have his grandparents.'

I thought that was a bit of a weird thing to say, why did he not just say his mother and father.

While we were showing each other everything, slowly removing my own clothes—while we were sharing secrets—to show him the rest of my own scars on my arms and my shoulders. All places where my clothes covered the pain and the hurt, where Edward had known nobody would see.

'You still love your husband's memory, even though he did all this to you? That's a statement not a question by the way.' He added, 'It's okay to still remember good things despite the bad.

I was silent for a moment before I decided to talk about my true feelings.

'He was a good man before he went to war' I sighed, 'I loved him since I was Seventeen years old. 'He came back from Dunkirk a stranger. Anything I said out of place in his mind ended in a beating.' I cried. 'I still loved the man he was before he went away.'

Jerold just simply put an arm around me and listened.–'I didn't blame him. 'I stiffened, 'I thought it was the war that changed him from a good man into a wife-beater. I thought he would change, but maybe it was him all along, and the war just brought it out of him. I cried when he went back to the front line.' I paused sniffing and gulped hard and looked at Jerold wide-eyed. 'But I cried because I was happy he was away.'

'Maybe,' he sighed. 'The war changed many people, but in some, the horrors just brought out evil that was already there.'

'While many others like you came back from the war and went through things just as terrible as he did and don't choose to hurt the ones you love.'

He slowly replied, 'My wife was dead, so I could hardly hurt her even if I had gone crazy.'

I tried to cheer him up but opened my big mouth. 'Mary was a lucky lady to have you.'

'She didn't have me though, did she?' He groaned, 'Like Edward never really had you. She lost me, and she lost the chance to bring up our son and we lost her.'

'Well,' I said, starting to rebutton my blouse. 'I'm sorry you and Mary never got your happily ever after.'

He looked at me with big sad eyes. 'And I'm sorry you and Edward didn't get yours.'

There was a moment where we just leaned on each other and held each other's bodies. I don't know why we did this exactly. I suppose it was us just confirming that we would always be there for each other.

'You can trust me,' I whispered. 'Never to tell your mother and father about your scars and what happened to you.'

Suddenly Jerrold pulled back and glared at me. 'What do you mean you won't tell my parents?'

'Well,' I said as I smiled awkwardly, 'I just want you to know that they'll not hear your secret from me.'

He looked me up and down, then he said, confused, 'Well, you could hardly tell them because you don't know my mother and father.'

Revelations

What Jerrold had just told me obviously left me in deep shock.

So, were Mr and Mrs Smith not his mother and father? How could that possibly be possible? His name was Jerrold Smith, and he lived with them. Was there anything else I didn't know about him?

There was no time to ask as the door clicked, and there was the sound of Jenn coughing as she opened the door. I heard her mumbling one of her predictions about the future involving a world where all houses had indoor toilets.

Jenn had many crackpot theories about how the world would be in the future. According to Jenn, the future would involve us having telephones in our houses and we would have portable devices to listen to music. I thought she was thinking of a type of gramophone in a rucksack, but she wasn't far off the right idea.

Anyway, she was so busy rambling on and brushing snow off her, that she didn't notice we had been topless. In fact, I had no idea why Jenn was there at all, when she lived next to the pub and had no need to have come to the farm, which was a mile away. The reason she later gave was that she helped Jerrold support me as I was too drunk to walk.

So, the events of that day turned out to be different from my expectations. There was no mention of the ghostly goings-on at the school. This was mainly because Thomas came downstairs to find his father and was overjoyed to see both his father and teacher in the room.

Mr and Mrs Smith both laughed at the fact that we'd all got drunk and slept on the chair, and they invited Jenn and me to stay for breakfast. The snow was coming down hard, and I thought that as payment for my breakfast, I would help Jerrold and Mr Smith to get the animals fed. It'd been a long hard winter already, and even somebody like me who was uneducated in farming terms knew that things were a struggle.

The horses, cattle, pigs, and sheep were thin, and supplies of hay and other food were running low. I think they were grateful for my help. Some farmers were funny about women helping, but Mr Smith proudly told me that the land girls who helped during the war were the best workers he'd ever had. Unlike a lot of farms Green Lake Farm had both crops and livestock. Most farms had either one or the other.

So, when the hard work was done, I stayed for lunch, and after I helped wash up, I went through some extra schoolwork with Thomas as though it was an average Saturday. However, it was pointless because he'd worked so hard that he was now above the level of the others

I was still suffering very much with my cold, and the warmth of the fire helped. Jerrold very kindly brought me a blanket, and a pile of his hankies, and told me I was going to stay in the spare room again. He then had to pop into the village shop for supplies. He usually would have walked with fuel in very short supply, but due to the hard-falling snow he took the truck with Mr Smith.

When they came back, Mr Smith went out to check the animals and Jerrold came to sit with Thomas and me where I caught him with a fresh tin of tobacco for me, which promised to pay him for it

'We can talk about the thing now,' he smiled.

'What thing?' I shrugged, thinking it was not an appropriate time to talk about me wanting to kiss him.

'The thing I wanted to talk about last night before the other thing happened and we got drunk.'

'Okay, that thing' I nodded. 'But is it something for little ears?'

'Little ears were the ones who told me about it!' he said, looking a little shaky.

'Oh, so what is it all about Tommy?'

Thomas looked up at his dad and then slowly back to me. After a while, he spoke. 'The big girl behind the toilet never went away.' Jerrold caught my eye.

'You know she's not real, right, Tommy,' I smiled.

'She is real,' he protested. 'She told me her name is M and she is with me always.'

'Tommy, can you tell me where she is now?' I asked looking around the room nervously.

He shrugged his shoulders. 'She tells me she can see us here, but I only see her at the school because of the energy.'

Jerrold and I exchanged worried looks. 'What energy is that son?'

'The energy coming from all the children at the school. It's in the walls, and she uses it to show herself to me there, but she can't do it here.' He then added in a soft voice. 'She can't do it here because her energy here is only pain and sadness.'

I wiped my nose and took a sip of tea, looking at Jerrold again to get his approval before asking further.

'Is M nice, or is she nasty to you?'

He looked at his dad, before answering me. 'She is nice like you.' He smiled, 'She wants you to be the headmistress.' I hadn't told Thomas about my promotion.

'Well, I'm glad she approves.' I smiled.

'But she told me to give you a warning.' He said, in a suddenly much colder, much stiffer voice.

I looked to Jerrold, now concerned. He looked just as worried, especially after what'd gone on the previous evening.

'What did she say?' I trembled, wondering if this was all a joke and he was doing this as a wind-up, but I knew deep down he was not.

'She says two things...' he paused. 'Firstly, she says that in a few years, they will find out that smoking kills you, so she wants you to stop as soon as you can. And, she says that photograph you carry around with you is evil, and it's getting stronger and if you don't get rid of it, then it's going to cause some serious trouble for us all.'

Okay, now I was scared. I had thought he saw the same ghost that I saw, or thought I saw. I thought the M he had spoken of was M for Maria. How could he know that I was taking her with me everywhere? She was safely tucked away in my handbag with the photo of my husband.

I needed to get it out and ask Tommy what she meant. I slowly picked up my handbag and took out the picture of the girl who I was sure was called Maria.

She stared back at me from her frame, as always. Her expression looked like it had never changed, as though she had always been still and never spoken to me.

Trying to hold my nerve, I held it up to Tommy, and asked, 'Is this the photograph she is talking about, or is this the girl that speaks to you?' He never got to answer me, because there was a gruff shout from behind me. I could hear not only a raw of passion, but for the first time I heard pure uncontrolled anger in him. It shocked the living daylights out of me. The usually quiet Mr Smith bellowed,

'Judith, where in the goddam fiery pits of hell did you get THAT?

Time to go home

Jerrold and I spun around in surprise. Mr Smith was red, shaking with some sort of emotion. I couldn't tell if it was fear or anger, or if he was overcome with happiness and in shock because of it. His face was red, but I wasn't sure if the tear in his eye was of anger or sorrow.

'You give that bloody thing to me right now!'

Shaking with fear at his sudden angry outburst, tears began to fall down my face as I passed it to him. My hand shook too much, and she slipped from my grasp, and I dropped her, the glass in her frame shattering into a hundred pieces.

'Now look what you did to her!' He yelled.

I looked back at him, frozen and confused, but something else I saw terrified me more. It was a look in Jerrold's eye that I'd never seen in him before. I might not of been able to read the emotion in Mr Smith, but Jerrold was about to explode with anger, and he was looking at me. What had I done to anger him?

He took a step toward me, and I instinctively took three steps back to avoid him, tripping on the armchair, which had fallen to the floor, luckily not hitting anything vital. Tommy was looking on terrified, with a tear in his eyes as Jerrold rushed over to me calling, 'Judith, are you okay, sweetheart.'

I should have known Jerrold would never hurt me, but it was learnt behaviour from my past. He had been angry at Mr Smith, not me. He had not been intending to hit me, he was trying to hug me to protect me from Mr Smith's outburst. Jerrold took my hand and helped me to my feet, taking me in both arms, gripping me tight against him before speaking to Mr Smith over my shoulder.

The tone was even more terrifying by the control in his voice. He didn't even need to raise his voice to make it known just how angry he was with Mr Smith, and, by this time, Mrs Smith had come in.

'How can you shout at poor Judith after everything she's done for us,' he growled, 'And in front of the boy too. You will never know the pain this poor kind sweet loving woman has gone through. Yet she runs herself into the ground for the children of this village.'

Mr Smith stopped, and he gazed at me with an awkward look in his eye as though he had not meant to shout, then he crumpled to his knees and stared down at the photograph. He began to pick up the pieces of glass. Mrs Smith joined him on the floor, but she glared at him rather than the photograph as Mr Smith began to weep silently. Mrs Smith then glared at me as if to say, 'what have you done to make my poor husband cry?'

There were several awkward moments as Jerrold stood between them and me with his arm on my shoulders. Thomas, who had always been so close to his grandfather, looked at him as though he was terrified of him. He moved over to the side of the room where I stood with his father. He stood between us where I stood with tears forming in my own eyes.

Cleary the photograph of the girl, Maria, meant something to Mr Smith. Maybe it was not all in my head. What if the girl in the photograph, whatever her real name was, had lived here once? With everything I'd seen in the past few months, let alone the past few days, who knew what was real anymore?

Mr Smith took the picture out of the frame and brushed the glass away, then he held the thin cardboard print to his chest. He looked over to me, then he stood up slowly and came towards me with his hand outstretched.

He spoke to me in a hoarse voice, 'Om, Sorry, Judith, I was out or order,' he breathed. 'You are bonnie young mauver you are, and I shunna yelled.' What he meant was that I was a lovely young woman.

'I've not seen that picture in many years, and it brought back some...' He paused and wiped his eyes on his sleeve. 'It's been so many years since I saw that photograph, and I thought it was gone forever.'

'It's been at my house ever since I moved here.' I said quietly, 'I-I-I...' I paused, how could I say that I carried the picture around because I was a madwoman, and the photograph was my friend.

'I took it to school yesterday for a history lesson.' I lied. 'The children were asked to bring in old pictures to study clothing and such, and I thought she was a good example for what children wore in the early part of the century.'

Mr Smith nodded slowly, 'As okay, gull. It just took me by surprise. Been so long since I saw that I thought it was gone years ago.'

With everything that was going on and with Mr Smith's reaction, I connected what Thomas's ghost woman had told him along with everything that happened to me since I found the photograph. They said that Victoria Ashworth went mad talking to the photograph. I knew that I was going mad talking to it myself. All the visions I saw when I was alone and all the dreams and her trying to tell me something. What if I was just one in a long line of people who had encountered her? Although the things around us terrified me, I did not think the girl herself was going to cause me harm—just the madness associated with her.

What if Mr Smith had been one of her playmates? Or, what if he knew of more people who had fallen under her spell. Was he once under her spell? Did he know her?

Mr Smith looked around the room at us all and saw Tommy, the boy who he had brought lovingly up for most of his life looking at him with terror in his eyes, then he looked to his wife who was stunned, as though she had never seen him act like that before either. 'I need…' he shivered. 'I need to talk with my wife alone.'

Everyone nodded uneasily.

'I'm going home,' I said quietly, slipping my arm from around Jerrold to mop my tears.

'Me too,' he added, to which I laughed uneasily taking a cigarette, intending to smoke as I walked home to keep me warm in the snow. 'You live here, so how can you go home?'

'I meant to drive you home.' He smiled.

'But you weren't invited.' I snapped, having genuinely intended to be on my own, but I didn't intend to be rude, I just wanted to be alone because of the shock of being yelled at. Yet then I didn't want to be alone at all. He looked a little shocked, so I quickly changed my tune and smiled, saying softly. 'You don't need to be invited, let's go and leave these two to talk.'

'No hard feelings, please.' Mr Smith begged, offering his hand for me to shake.

I didn't take his hand. Instead, I hugged him just long enough to whisper in his ear so nobody else could hear '

'I know you're not the type of person to shout at a lady, especially me. There are hard feelings, but they will go away when you tell me why you got so upset and who Maria is to you.'

As I stepped away, he looked me in the eye with an expression of shock, which now proved in my mind that Maria was not a name I made up in my head.

The Scrabble board

Outside the snow was falling hard and the farm glistened in a blanket of white. While Jerrold got to work firing up the truck with the starter handle, I sat outside the barn on an upturned bucket, sucking on my cigarette as snow settled on my head. To be fair it was only my second cigarette of the day despite the time being 4 p.m.

Tommy came out of the house carrying a small bag of clothes. Clearly, he was intending not to be returning tonight. I didn't have the heart to tell them that there weren't enough beds in my house for one of them to stay over—let alone both—and I had been expecting them both to go home after I fed them and gave Mr and Mrs Smith some time to talk.

'Are you okay, Judith?' He asked, seeing me sat there.

I nodded slowly as I took a last drag and put my cigarette out on the snow, seeing that it hissed and steamed. Then I blew my nose with a honk.

'I'll live,' I grinned, '…but what about you?' He was shaking with either cold or fear.

'I don't like it when Grandad shouts.' He quivered.

There were times when it was okay to break the teacher-pupil rules, and now was one of those times. I stuffed the handkerchief in my coat pocket and put my arms out to him. I hugged that little boy tight into me. He didn't have a mum for these moments, and I didn't want to take her place, but his teacher and family friend wanted to be there for him. Plus, it was partly somehow my fault he got scared. In that instant, part of me also thought hugs like this were only the tip of the iceberg when it came to things I was missing out on by choosing not to pursue the chance of having my own children.

'Judith, 'He said in my ear after a good few moments of hugging. 'What is it, Tommy?'

I shouldn't have asked. These things had a habit of slipping out of young mouths. He pulled away to look me in the eye, but he held my arms with a cheeky grin.

'You smell of sweat, beer, and cigarettes.'

I smiled back at him apologetically.

'Sometimes, us grown-ups need to relax, and we need to play just like children do, but we play in different ways, and sometimes that causes us to end up in unexpected places without clean clothes.'

He winked at me.

'You, Dad, and Miss Spelling—he was referring to Jenn—all got drunk and fell asleep on each other.' He smiled, then he did and said something that melted my heart. He braved my apparent disgusting smell and gave me another hug saying, 'I'm glad you got to have fun. I love you, Aunty Judith. I pulled him closer into me and as I smiled, I looked up to see Jerrold with the starting handle in hand, grinning at us both proudly.

No words were said, we just got up and made our way to the truck with Tommy holding my hand.

We had to stop off at the shop to buy food because I was a single woman living alone and didn't have enough food for three of us. A few years later that would not be a problem, but with the rationing system, we were lucky that the Smiths had not already bought their week's food as they would not be allowed any more.

The snow was what we expected from winter these days. The road must have been covered in a couple of inches which was nothing compared to what was to come in the weeks that followed.

It was slow going, and it was beginning to get dark by the time we made it back to my cottage. Although Jerrold was staying for dinner, he still had work to do on the farm making sure the animals were safe from the snow and that the barns were secure. Unsure whether Mr Smith was in the correct mental or physical state to carry out these jobs alone, Jerrold took the truck back leaving Tommy and me to get dinner. Jerrold of course being the forerunner of the modern man unbelieving of now outdated views, wanted to make it clear that a woman's place was not in the kitchen.

To this, I responded, 'It is if you want dinner when you get back. Now get going.'

He gave me a quick one-arm hug, then he left. A sort of awkward thanks for letting us come with me and for watching his son type hug.

I kept Tommy busy helping me to clear out the dead fire from the grate and make a new one. We could see our breath in front of our faces. I could see the headlines now if we didn't warm the place up. Seven-year-old freezes to death in headteacher's house. Good way to lose your job before your official first day.

Tommy might have been behind when it came to schoolwork, but that boy was good when it came to practical things like fire lighting, probably from doing it at home. We had it laid out and ready to light in only a few minutes. We were missing something vital. Matches, the pack on the mantelpiece was empty. I felt in my pocket, but all that was there was my purse and a used handkerchief. Without them we were stuck for heat.

Tommy went out to use the toilet while I continued to look. Then it hit me. I put the matches in my handbag with my tobacco.

'Thank God I'm a smoker,' I thought. I knew I shouldn't say that. I went over to the table. I took out the photograph of Edward, intending to do what I should have done a long time ago and hide the blasted thing away, but I jumped back in fright.

I trembled as every hair on my body, bar the ones on my head, stood on end. Back at the farmhouse, I had walked away leaving the photograph of Maria with Mr Smith as its frame lay smashed on the floor. Yet, by an impossible dark twist of terrifying magic, it was there. It was back in my handbag as though I had never taken it out at the farm.

I was still stood there shaking when Tommy came in from the toilet, covered in snow. The warning from Tommy's ghost was still fresh in my mind. He told me, she said it was evil and I had to get rid of it. But how could I get rid of it? Just how did it put itself back together and get back in my handbag. Seeing Tommy coming, I quickly hid it back in my bag.

I struggled to keep hold of my emotions, turning towards the fireplace speaking to him with my back turned. Tommy was already dealing with the fact that he saw ghosts, he didn't need this added to that, and neither did I.

With a flick of a match, the fire promptly... did nothing and the flame burned out in seconds. It took me three or four attempts with several bits of the balled-up paper before the kindling started to catch. Finally, amber flames rose wafting heat towards me, warming my hands and face as I beckoned Tommy to come and warm himself.

Once I'd prepared dinner to the point that it would just need heating up when Jerrold joined us, I looked around for something to keep Tommy entertained. Just because I was a teacher, that did not mean I had anything for children in my home. I didn't have a television and none of my books were suitable. What I did have though was Jenn's Scrabble board which she'd left at my house, because I was the only person who'd give her a game of it.

A game of Scrabble would be good for the pair of us. It would help Tommy with his English, and it would keep my mind off what was going on and what was in my handbag. I put the kettle on the hob for a cup of tea, and we set the board out on the table. I was rather enjoying myself making Tommy think he was beating me at it.

It also gave us time to have a chat about things in a way that teachers and pupils didn't usually get to do. I asked Tommy what he thought about me being headmistress and teaching the older children permanently. At first, he was disappointed that I wasn't going back to teach his class, but then he beamed a smile at me, when I explained this meant he would be having me for much longer than he would have done if I'd stayed.

'I wish you were my mummy.' He said quietly.

That kind of shocked me. I didn't know what to say to it. What did you say to a child who never knew their parent?

The best I could do was to say. 'Your mummy will always be your mummy. She would have been a great mummy and she didn't want to go to heaven, but she has other people there like me. There are people like your grandparents and me who are helping your dad because your mummy can't.'

'Thanks, Aunty Judith. I love you,' he grinned.

I returned the smile, then blew my nose. At least the drama of that afternoon had taken my mind off feeling ill. Painkillers and cold relief were not easily available in those days.

'Love you too, little man.' I sniffed, 'But, remember at school, Mrs Johnston. And don't say you love me at school because your classmates might laugh, and I might get sacked.'

I hoped Jerrold would be back soon. I worried about him out there, driving in the dark in the snow. I worried more about Jerrold's safety driving the truck in the snow than I worried about my husband Edward on D-Day when he faced the might of the Nazi monster with all the other young men.

I felt bad for thinking that because I did love Eddy. Whatever kind of monster he became when he was on shore leave, he fought and lost his life for the freedom of those of us at home, just like many did. I was devastated when he died. I had been going to give him a chance to change, but part of me knew all along that when he came back from the war it would most likely end in a messy divorce.

Without warning, the kitchen light went out leaving us in the dark.

While I jumped out of my skin, Tommy shrieked out with fright.

Thankfully the flickering light of the fire meant it was not complete blackness. Still, it was dark enough that Tommy didn't want to be left alone.

He followed me to the drawer where thankfully there was one light bulb left. I used what light there was from the fire to move the armchair into position under the lampshade. I kept Tommy busy, leading him to the light switch and turning it off and told him to flick it on when I said. I fumbled in the dark standing on the chair for a few minutes before trying to click the bulb in.

There was a sudden screech in the dark that made me jump back off the chair, almost falling to the cold hard floor pulling the light bulb with me. My heart raced, and I breathed hard. It was just the kettle boiling, I forgot I had put it on for a cup of tea.

I rushed over to turn the kettle off and went back to the chair, where I finally managed to click the light in successfully. Tommy flicked the switch, and there was a blinding flash of light. A person who wasn't stupid would not have been looking at the bulb when he turned it on. The light was brighter than I thought it would be and it burned my eyes, and I stumbled. A sudden bang at the door made me jump once more and I fell, this time on my backside, I sat dazed on the floor. I remembered hearing Tommy shout that it was his dad at the door.

I was still sitting on the floor looking stupid when Jerrold, who was covered in snow, bent down to me, offering his hand.

'You okay, clumsy? What are you doing down there?'

'Considering I'm supposed to be a headteacher I'm doing a very bad job of looking after your son.'

He laughed when I told him about the light bulb as he pulled me to my feet.

'We've been having lots of fun,' Tommy said quickly.

I smiled, 'You should see the amazing words he's been spelling while I go and heat dinner.'

I was almost at the cooker when Jerrold called to me. 'Judith, you need to come and see this.'

I hurried over to see what he wanted. He was pointing at the Scrabble board with his mouth drooping slightly. I looked down to see the game we had been playing was no longer there. The letters were spread out in a message, and it was not a message that I would want Tommy to see. It used a word that for 1947 was considered by most to be too vulgar to say.

'Fuck you, Kathleen. Jerrold Smith is a killer, I'm coming for you. '

A drink with Jerrold

'Tommy, did you do this?' I shrieked. He looked up at me with that terrified face he had shown when his grandad had yelled earlier. He was as terrified as me and what was worse was that I knew there was no way he could have done it. Immediately before he could run, I dropped to my knees, and I hugged him tightly to me and apologised the best I could for yelling, then told him that I knew he couldn't have done it.

I flinched as Jerrold moved towards me. I thought he was going to be angry because I shouted at Tommy, but Jerrold was taken aback and looked shocked. I thought he was going to use violence. When I saw the awkward look, he gave me, I smiled weakly and let him join us in our hug.

The cottage still hadn't fully warmed. There was still a chill in the air, but I was dripping in sweat like I'd run a marathon. I didn't know what to do or think. I went over to the cooker and turned on the heat to warm our dinner. Then I told Tommy I needed his dad's help to draw more water from the well. It was an excuse to go outside with Jerrold alone.

I picked up my bag on the way past. Once outside, I lit up a cigarette and asked Jerrold. 'Do you think whatever did that to the Scrabble letters is the same thing that was at the school last night?'

'I'm not sure,' he quivered. 'None of this seems real. How can it be? Ghosts don't exist. There has to be some other explanation for it, but what?'

'I know.' I breathed. 'I wouldn't blame you for thinking I wrote that myself, but we both heard Tommy talk about his ghost at the school. She said the photograph was evil. What if it's her that's doing this?'

But how could it be if she was? She had saved me and calmed me down after the vision I had of the singing children all those months ago. The girl I saw when I dreamed of her was not evil. She was not right. she seemed to have a severe mental impairment. That must be the reason she couldn't attend school, but she was kind, not violent in any way. Yet Tommy's ghost who he knew only as M said the photograph was bad. I couldn't disagree about something that could break into pieces and put itself back together.

The snow was coming down hard. Rather than struggle as far as the well, we gathered some snow into a bucket to melt on the stove.

'Jerrold,' I said softly and nervously, reaching into my handbag before we got back to the cottage.

'What is it?'

I used the dim light of my cigarette to show him the photograph of Maria in my hand. I couldn't see his face, but I heard him breathe deeply in shock.

'You took it back from him. You put it in another frame. You must have done it. This is all a trick.'

'It's not.' I yelled over the wind, 'It was in my handbag when I got the matches for the fire. I swear when I left the farmhouse it was still inside with no frame.'

• • •

'After what I saw last night.' He breathed, 'I find it hard not to believe you. Especially after what happened with Jerrold senior this afternoon. He must know something about that picture.

Again, I wonder why he had called Mr Smith, Jerrold Senior, but then I remembered back to the conversation that morning when he mentioned the Smiths not being his parents.

We didn't want to leave Tommy alone in the room too long, so we agreed to discuss things further once he was in bed. That of cause proved a problem, because I didn't really have the room for one person to sleep over let alone two. Even when Jenn stayed over, she slept in my bed with me, but it wasn't like Jerrold was going to stay in my bed. That still left Tommy, but we could sort something.

It was already eight o'clock by the time we finished dinner, so Tommy went straight to my bed while Jerrold and I cracked open the bottle of whisky that the late Mr Robinson gave me for Christmas, and we sat sipping by the fire in the armchairs.

We calmly talked over everything that went on at the meeting the night before. Not the school stuff but the table lifting and the typewriter typing on its own.

Once we were finished talking about the previous night, I looked over at Jerrold and took a big gulp of whisky and said quietly. 'Maybe you'll think I'm crazy, but I need to tell you everything.'

So, I did.

I began with everything that'd happened when I came to the village —finding the photograph waiting for me, how the matches had fallen out of the packet and formed an arrow pointing at her, how I'd had the dream and woken to find the word "hell" next to the photograph. I told him details of the dreams of Maria sat alone, playing by herself at the farm. Her longing to be allowed to go to the school and her lack of understanding of why she couldn't.

I told him how I'd recognised the farm the night I first went there to meet with him but hadn't wanted to say for fear of him thinking I was crazy. I told him about the visions of my husband dead in the chair, the children singing to me and rotting to death before my eyes.

'I thought it might have been her who trashed the house and left that nasty message...' I breathed. 'Yet, in the dreams, she seems so innocent and childlike, and she just wants someone to talk to when she's lonely, so I talk to her when there's nobody here.'

I told him how, despite no longer being lonely now I had him and his family and Jenn, I had continued to carry her around and tell her everything that was going on.

He sat there and listened calmly without a word until I recapped everything to do with the photograph and the things that'd happened at the school. How I'd wondered if she was the girl that Tommy had been seeing.

'And now I don't know what to think. She might be jealous of my friendship with you and Jenn, now that it's not just her and me.'

Jerrold looked at me, but he remained silent.

'Maybe,' I sighed, looking over at the Scrabble board now packed away in the corner. 'Maybe she's trying to break our friendship by leaving messages like that on the board, so that I don't want to spend time with you anymore.'

'You think I'm crazy, don't you?'

He looked at me, but he paused before he spoke. 'I don't think you're crazy.' He said simply, 'The world works in so many strange ways.'

'I talk to a photograph and pretend she replies, and you don't think I'm crazy?'

Jerrold glanced at me, but then looked away before speaking softly. 'When I was in the camp, I was put into solitary confinement for a month.' He told me, before another small sip of whisky, and looking at me sideways before staring into the fire. 'The only thing that kept me sane was talking to George and Melvin.'

'I'm sorry that happened to you.' I sighed, in the silence, wiping my nose while I digested what he said before speaking. 'SOOO, solitary confinement, you were on your own in a cell, right? But with George and Melvin?'

He nodded as a small smile crossed his face. 'George was a piece of wood and Melvin was a dead slug, but to me they were friends.' I smiled at him uneasily.

'I can't imagine how horrifying that must've been.' I breathed.

'Maddening.' He shrugged quietly. 'So weak and thin and so hungry. So many real friends were dying every day of starvation and all sorts of diseases.'

'You poor man. You made up friends to get away from it all.' I whispered. 'But you made it, you're alive, and you really have friends now.'

He reached over and put his hand on my shoulder, 'And so I have in you.'

For a moment I just sat there and let him touch me, but then I sat up straight. Maybe he was right. Maybe I did make Maria up in my head because I was lonely, but there was more than that.

'Look,' I told him bluntly in a rant. 'I know you're trying to help me, and I adore you and Tommy. Meeting you is the best thing that's happened to me in a long time. Maybe part of me did feel lonely and wanted to invent a new friend or something to keep my brain active while I was lonely. Maybe Tommy and his friend M are just the same. But you can't deny what we saw last night or what's been going on at the school. Plus, Mr Smith clearly knew her, and he had something private to tell Mrs Smith.'

I paused for a breath and sneezed before going on. 'And another thing, right? You live with Mr and Mrs Smith, and I thought they were your parents, but you said I never met your parents, so what's the deal there?'

Jerrold calmly put his hand up to stop me ranting and waited patiently for me to take a deep breath.

'I believe you.' He said simply. 'Maybe you did invent a friend in your head because you were lonely, but that doesn't explain everything. It can't explain last night, and it can't explain how a broken photograph put itself together or the messages. And as for Mr and Mrs Smith not being my parents, I just didn't realise that you didn't already know.'

He took a deep breath and asked my permission to pour himself another glass of my whisky, to which I smiled and indicated he should fill mine too.

'It's a simple story, really. I live with the Smiths because that's where Tommy lives.'

He went on to tell me that he had moved to the farm to work as a live-in farmhand when he was fifteen. He was living and working there, and that was how he ended up falling head over heels in love with their eldest daughter.

'Obviously, if you've been following the story, that was Tommy's mother, Mary.'

'So I married her very young, and in a rush much like you did with Edward. Mary and I had lived in part of the farm building rather than get our own home. So, of course when I was away in Japan and Mary passed away, then it was natural that her parents took on Tommy's care until I returned.'

There was no animosity between him and his own parents. When Mr and Mrs Smith referred to Jerrold as their son, they simply meant son-in-law. Tommy was given the Smith's surname, and Jerrold's surname was Willmott, not Smith.

We laughed at the fact I'd known him for nearly seven months and not known his surname.

So that was why he hadn't been at all concerned that the words on the board had accused him of being a killer. He wasn't Jerrold Smith so wasn't the accused. That was his former farther in-law. I couldn't think of him as a killer. Whatever wrote that message was evil and maybe wanted me to think he could be. But then I remembered the anger in his eye's when he saw the photograph. Perhaps just perhaps it was telling the truth. This left a question, what happened to Maria?

It was hard to date the photograph. It could have been anywhere from between 1900 and 1915 making Maria roughly (Had she lived) between Forty-two and Fifty- seven-years-old. What if she was trying to tell us that Jerrold Smith killed her? But why would she talk about herself in third person?

'So, getting back to this photograph,' Jerrold continued after a huge yawn, stretching his arm and laying it around my shoulders.

'I think Jerry reacting like that means he must have known her. Very possible, seeing as he was born there.'

'Hang on,' I said. Suddenly, with excitement flashing across my face in the firelight. 'Mr Smith is Jerry. Maria's brother in the dreams was called Jay, but that's not right though, is it? She wasn't well, her speech wasn't good. She called him Jay because she couldn't pronounce Jerry.'

He stared at me as though he wasn't quite getting it, then it suddenly clicked.

'You m-mean...' he stammered, standing up to get the picture from where I left it on the table. I nodded and smiled. 'Maria was a real person, and she was Mr Smith's big sister.'

'And not only that.' He grinned, looking at the picture in the light of the fire. 'She's Tommy's great aunt.' He paused to look at me. 'What if his friend M is Maria? She's the ghost of his great aunt coming back to help him.'

'Of course.' I breathed, with my heart suddenly racing. 'And she haunts the school, she communicates with teachers like me because she never could when she was alive.'

I was about to add that the girl who brought the picture into school was Mary. That must have been Tommy's mum Mary. Though she would goon to marry him, Jerrold wasn't in her class wasn't in her class being two years older. I doubt mr Robinson had ever shown the photograph to his students either that's why he never saw it.

Bang! Something crashed behind us. We both jumped in shock, looking around to see what it was. Jerrold grabbed my arm tight. We looked around by the light of the fire, but we saw nothing, so I put the light on—still nothing.

Bang, bang, bang, bang, bang.

I put my hand on my rushing heart. Nothing to worry about. Just some poor person out in the snow banging on my door at almost midnight. That seemed quite normal.

Jerry Smith

As I approached the door, I felt Jerrold's arm around my shoulder as though he wished to support me in case the person outside was some sort of hostile. Although I didn't need his arm there, it was comforting to know I had support. It was probably the neighbours coming to tell us to stop talking and get to bed.

As the door opened, I saw a figure dressed in a thick coat and hood standing in the doorway. He was covered in snow and was coughing heavily and said in a croaking voice. 'I believe you have something of mine.'

He shook the snow from his coat and cleared his throat as he stepped into my home, uninvited. I was looking around me to find something to hit the man with. Then suddenly I stopped and laughed with embarrassment as he pulled his hood back.

'Mr Smith.' I breathed.

'Can I ask you a question?' He smiled awkwardly.

'Ask away while I put the kettle on and pour you something alcoholic.' I smiled, turning towards the kettle.

'She's had a bit of a shock, and a lot of whisky,' Jerrold warned him.

'Why do you always call me. Mr Smith and not Jerry?'

I stopped stunned at the question, before blurting out. 'Okay, well I suppose you're both called Jerrold it's just it's just easier.

'You forgot my name dint ya gul?

'Might have done.' I confessed.

Both he and Jerrold roared out laughing.

'It's not funny.' I scolded them both. 'Think how silly I am and then remember you got me appointed as the headteacher of your son's school.'

As he could probably tell—the amount of alcohol that both Jerrold and I had consumed was hitting us.

'This thing of yours that I have?' I grinned, picking up the photograph from the table and passing it to him.

He looked at it, surprised to see it reframed and gave me a confused look.

'Among my limited skills are gluing things and putting broken glass back together.' I lied unconvincingly.

I couldn't exactly tell him. 'Oh yeah, I just found it completely fixed in my handbag after leaving it in your house. Oh yeah, and apparently, according to the Scrabble board, You're a murderer.'

He looked at me and at the picture, and he smiled and put it down on the table awkwardly.

'When I said you got something of mine, I was talking about my truck. Am gonna need it tomorrow.'

'You knew I was bringing it back in the morning so tell us the reason you walked nearly two miles in snow in the dead of night?' Jerrold demanded.

'Come on, sit down,' I told him, showing him to my armchair and handing him a glass of whisky to warm him, as he must've been freezing.

'Where are you sitting?' Jerrold asked, to which I replied,

'In your seat!'

'Where am I sitting then?' he continued.

'Also, in your seat, so I can keep you warm,' I told him with confidence I wouldn't of had, had I not been tipsy.

I don't know why, but I picked up Maria and moved her from the dining table and put her on the mantlepiece above the fire. In my mind, I thought I was wanting her to see what was being said about her. It was silly. She was just a photograph of a child. She didn't really speak. Even if she was Jerry's sister, I was sure the dreams had been all made up in my head.

I put another couple of logs on the fire, poured the tea, then I switched out the main light and squeezed my pudgy bottom into the armchair next to Jerrold, who put his arm around me. I put my left arm around him and held my handkerchief in my right hand, letting it drop over the side to avoid getting my germs too close.

'I had to have a little chat with my wife,' Jerry told us. 'To make her understand what made me snap like that.'

'We did all wonder because you never shout and you are a brilliant grandad to Tommy,' Jerrold assured him.

'It ain't easy telling your wife of thirty years something like that when she had no idea about it, but once it was off my chest after all these years, I couldn't sleep without telling you both the truth. Just lucky you pair weren't in bed.'

'We aren't sleeping together!' Jerrold and I both said together.

'I dint say you was.' He added with a smile. 'But there's not much about you two to suggest I'd be wrong if I thought you were.'

Jerrold and I looked at each other, as if we both intended to deny our closeness by removing our arms from around each other. but in the end, we somehow ended up getting even closer.

'So, you want to tell me what you know about the girl in the picture?' I asked Jerry, who was sitting to my left on the other side of Jerrold.

'I do.' He smiled, and I nodded, but Jerrold raised a hand and stopped him.

'Before you tell us you need to listen to Judith. That way, if what she's told me about it is what's happened, then she can't be accused of basing it on what you say.'

'Good thinking you.' I smiled.

'Not often we say that about Jerrold.' Jerry teased.

I took another sip of whisky, blew my nose and took a huge gulp of tea and told Jerry every little detail that had happened up to that moment including the warnings from Tommy's ghost friend, M and the Scrabble board.

The reall Maria

Jerry listened quietly without a word as I told him everything I knew, including the dreams and how Jenn had said talking to the picture had driven Vicky Ashworth to kill herself, and how
we thought the threats were coming through the photograph.

When I finished, I went to put the kettle on once more and use the outhouse, then went upstairs to check on Tommy, and I could get a clean handkerchief from my dressing table. Something on my dressing table caught my eye. It was the music box—Maria's music box.

When I came down, Jerrold had already made us more tea, but Jerry was sat looking into the fire thoughtfully. He waited patiently.

'There are many, many things in this world that I can never get my head around.' He sniffed. 'I've listened to everything. You must be telling the truth to know these things. I think the word I've heard for it is paranormal. Something like that anyway.'

'So, it's all true then. Maria was really her name, and she was your sister?'

He nodded, but his head dropped to his hands.

One of the most horrible things to see in life was when a person who had lived a great deal of it, was still feeling so low that it drove them to tears.

After a moment, he composed himself.

'She was my sister.' He confirmed, 'And her name was Maria, but things you've seen happening were so long ago. I was young myself, and memories get twisted. I think what you saw was the world as she saw it. To everyone outside the family, and even some inside as you saw with my grandmother, Maria was the village idiot, but to most of the family she was just Maria, and we loved her even though she could be very angry towards our mother and father.'

When I asked him if she had a diagnosis for her problems, he looked at me and I thought he was going to laugh. 'Modern medication has come a long way, but I don't think medication can help her problems. Even now you can't just go to the doctor like this fantasy idea for nationalising health care that they're talking about starting up.

To me,' he continued. 'We were all family and non-perfect, and my sister was my sister. I loved her and wanted the best for her just like my other siblings, if not her more. Despite what she seems to have thought, our parents loved her. She loved me most and knew mother and father loved her, but she couldn't always understand.'

I nodded, 'She blamed them for things outside their control because she thought they controlled everything in the world because they were her mother and father. Toddlers think their parents are in charge of the world, but whatever was wrong with her stopped her reaching the mental capacity to realise that isn't how the world works.'

'I think you hit the nail there.' He agreed.

'From what I saw of her thoughts.' I sighed, 'I think she was intelligent enough to realise that she was not as bright as others, and that was eating away at her.'

'Again, nail on the head' He sighed, 'She was not stupid, far from it. Give her a globe, and she could name every country on it. Give her a canvas or a sheet of paper, and she could paint a masterpiece. Like you saw, she could create something real from a photograph without having it in front of her. Yet,' he said, wiping away a tear. 'She couldn't tie her own shoes, or wipe her own nose, couldn't read, couldn't write, and her speech was a long way behind, and she interacted with other kids poorly.'

'I guess they stopped her going to school because it wasn't fair to her when she couldn't cope with it.'

'Can't you tell you're a teacher?' He smiled weakly.

The basis of the conversation was that what Maria needed was a special school that could help her cope with her problems with others like her.

Years later we have such schools with a much better understanding of the mentally challenged, but Maria was born in the wrong time, and the wrong place, so she got nothing, but a lack of help and respect as a person.

I was no expert of course, but I was almost one hundred per cent sure that what Maria was suffering from was a reasonably severe case of autism and possibly hyperactivity. It would become very commonly known and if she'd been a child these days, she would have been given all the help she needed at school. But even then, in 1947 there was no way as a teacher that I could offer one to one lessons full time. Yet, who knew? She might have just needed extra help like I gave Tommy. She would need it to a much heavier degree, but it would've done her the world of good instead of sitting home alone with no friends, rotting away.

'That photograph if memory serves me write was taken in 1907. Only well-off families like ours could afford such a thing. My Nan did love Maria, but in them days you had to stand still for it to work. Nan didn't think Maria could stand still enough, tha's why she had her removed. Doesn't excuse what the old cow said or did.' He paused to sip his tea.

'Grandad felt so bad that he paid the photographer a lot of money to come back to take another picture. Luck had that he'd already taken that one. She took it everywhere with her until she left us.'

'May I ask, when she died?' I asked softly.

'You may.' He shrugged, 'But you may not get an answer seeing as I don't know any details of when, where, or how...' He paused,

'... because last time I saw her she was twenty-two-years-old. It was 1917 almost thirty-years ago. She was being sentenced to twenty years in prison for the murder of my father a year earlier. She only escaped being hung for it because she clearly wasn't capable of knowing what she was doing. The judge took pity on her.

'She murdered your father?' I gasped.

Jerrold and I looked at each other open-mouthed. You could here a pin drop as I struggled to see Jerry's face in the light from the embers of the fire.

After a ' silence, he shook his head. 'No! No she did not, but she did the time for it. But that's a story for another night.'

The winter of 47

We must have got so drunk that we fell asleep. When I awoke, I was lying by the fireplace under mine and Jerrold's coats, because Tommy had the only covers upstairs.

We all went back to the farm that morning and Maria's photograph came with us. I enjoyed helping out on the farm in my spare time.

With 1947 being a very cold winter already with snow everywhere, I felt my help on the farm would be appreciated.

That night after we'd all said goodnight, Jerrold and I caught each other trying to tiptoe into each other's rooms. I guessed we were both pretending we had something to tell the other. We didn't get much sleep, and on Monday I went into work looking like a zombie.

In the early hours of Tuesday the 21st of January, we awoke to a loud banging on the bedroom door. It was early and I was still in bed with Jerrold. I hadn't woken early enough to creep into the spare room. There was nowhere to hide in the room apart from the wardrobe. I didn't know why we wanted to hide our relationship, but somehow the timing didn't seem right. But then Mr Smith's voice came through the door.

'Don't worry, Judith, we all know you're sleeping with Jerrold. We're all adults and there's nothing wrong with it. Please get up, we need your help. We have a problem outside.'

He sounded so urgent that both of us were up and dressed in a matter of seconds, and we were out of the door and downstairs. It was still dark outside, but in the light from the living room window, we could see the snow coming down faster than I'd ever seen in my life. We could hear the wind howling all around the house.

Jerry Smith was stood in the doorway in his thick coat, and he was white from head to foot in ice and snow. 'What's up Jerry?' Jerrold asked him, without hesitation.

'The darn storm has taken out the east wall of the barn. Cows escaped. They're all over the farm.'

Jerrold was already putting on his thick farming coat. 'Right,' He said, 'We need to move anything and everything out of the shed and use it as a temporary barn. It'll be a squeeze but we have to save as many as possible.'

'That's the best plan,' Mr Smith shouted over the wind. 'But have you seen how deep the snow is out there? We'll have to dig them out. Even with the two of us, it'll be hours before we can even dig out enough snow to move the stuff from the sheds. By then the cows could be all over the village.'

'What do you mean two people,' I asked, pulling on my gloves and hat. 'Which one of you two is staying here?'

'But Judith you're…' Mr Smith started.

'I have arms and legs, and I know how to use a shovel,' I told him bluntly. 'The fact that I'm a woman is irrelevant.'

He smiled, 'If you let me finish, I was gonna say. You're wearing a skirt, so go and put on a pair of Jerrold's trousers and I'll find you a thicker coat and boots from what the girls left behind.'

I hadn't thought of the fact that he would've had land girls on the farm. During the war, when all the young men like Jerrold had been off fighting. The government sent out an army of women to help run the farms and keep the country fed. I didn't know they had them at Green Lake Farm though. But I should have done because I remember him telling me now.

I rushed upstairs to change. When I came back down, we were joined by Mrs Smith.

I'd never been so cold in my whole life. The door to the tool shed was blocked with snow, and we had to dig with our hands to get the door open to get the shovels for more digging. We had two pressure lamps on the go either side of the door. The snow was already three or four feet deep in places, and the more we dug into it, the more fell. The pain in my arms and legs from digging was unreal. I'd never felt burning and exhaustion like it. Cold and sweating all at the same time.

At a rough guess of the time, it took us, I'd say it was two hours before we managed to get the door open. Things from then would be a little simpler, or so we thought. Mr Smith's tractor was thankfully fitted with a scoop.

He fired up the tractor and moved it around the truck and rammed it at the snowdrift, before lifting what he could of the snow over to the side of the cleared area. Even with us still digging alongside the plough it must've been a further hour before we had the space to start moving things out of the shed, let alone start rounding up the cattle which would be impossible as the snow was now so high that in one place it was above my head.

The situation was becoming dire. Jerrold started up the truck and moved it out into the clear space behind the tractor.

Jerrold explained to me that the amount of stuff in the shed was down to the farm being one of the rare farms that dealt in both livestock and arable farming, so unlike other farms, they needed equipment for both. At the moment they had to cope with only two people running the farm, as the two casual labourers from the village who also worked on the farm, were safe at home with their own families.

Behind the truck was all sorts of stuff. Between us, we dragged out the heavy plough that went with the tractor. Behind that was a threshing machine. Further back was some stuff that interested me even further. It was stuff that I'd seen in my dreams. The hay cart that broke down outside the school with Maria on it. It'd been there so long that it was rusted, and Jerrold had to use the truck to pull it out of the way. Behind that and leaned up against the wall was the small rowing boat with faded words painted on it, HMS Maria.

By the time all of the equipment was moved, it was light outside.

Light, but not light as the snow was still falling thick and fast.

Even the men were not used to the level of physical work we'd all just put ourselves through. We all needed a quick rest and a warm-up before going back out into the storm. We all went back to the house and warmed ourselves by the fire and being British we needed tea. Now there was only the task of finding thirty huge milk cows and trying to stop them from freezing to death.

Hours passed as we searched the farm trying to keep in touch with each other by shouting over the wind. By this time the two farmhands from the village had realised there might be a situation and come to help. After a long search we came across most of the herd in the far-field by the lake. Many of them were panicked or stuck. I didn't know how we did it, but with six of us working our socks off we managed it.

We were not cowboys although we did have ropes. The horses on the farm were stuck in their stables, so we used a human chain to round up the cows, with dogs helping and finally, twenty-eight out of the thirty were in the shed. Sadly, the other two were found dead.

Then the rest of the animals, including horses' pigs and sheep which were already in the other barns had to be fed. It took more digging to get the doors open.

It was already starting to get dark. It had been around three o'clock in the morning that Mr Smith had woken us. My first thoughts upon seeing that it was now 3 p.m. was to say, 'Shit I just missed work. I mean, oh gosh, darn it, I missed work.'

Jerrold laughed, 'I think school might be closed today, Mrs Johnston.'

'That's Miss Johnston to you.' I winked, 'Now we're in a new relationship. I don't think Mrs Is appropriate.

He smiled and kissed me gently. 'Thank you for your help today. You were amazing.' He whispered, to which I replied, 'We're family.'

'Speaking of which, I need to go and get Tommy. The poor kid's been in his room all day.'

A few moments later, Jerrold came rushing downstairs in a panic.

'Did Tommy come down? Has anyone seen him?'

'No not seem him all day.'

'Tommy you here, boy?'

We were shouting and searching the house for many minutes to no avail, when all of a sudden, something caught my eye.

The photograph of Maria was on the table in the living room where Tommy, Jerrold and I had been playing Scrabble the night before. Some of the letters from the Scrabble set were in front of it with a badly spelt sentence, which made me yell for Jerrold.

'Tommy went school M.'

I picked up the photo as Jerrold came running and saw the message.

'Did you write this here, Maria?'

I asked her, not expecting a reply and not caring if Jerrold thought I was crazy. I was about to shove it back into my bag when suddenly her lips moved, and a voice came out of them.

'Playmate, Judith. Tommy w-went s-school find-d M-Mary. He in ddanger and s-s-so are you?'

Then she went flat and back to being just a normal photograph.

'I always thought you were a little crazy, but I loved you, anyway.' Jerrold trembled behind me. 'But if you're crazy, then it must have rubbed off on me because I just saw that too.

A child in the school

We were exhausted and hungry having been working for so many hours in the cold. We would happily have gone to bed and slept for an hour then and there, but nobody had thought to watch Tommy. Nobody would have thought that he would have any reason to go anywhere. We couldn't explain to Mr and Mrs Smith why we thought he was at school, because Mrs Smith would think we were mad. Mr Smith knew we weren't.

Luckily the wind direction meant the front of the house was sheltered so that the snow only built up at the back, so the front door was clear at least. Mrs Smith and the two farmhands went out to check around the farm. Jerrold and I and Mr Smith made our way along the route he would have taken to the school.

What on earth he was doing going to the school, and how he even thought he could get there was beyond me. There was no reason for any of it. All I could think of was that it was something to do with M whoever M was. Why would Maria want a little boy to be at the school in this awful blizzard? There was no way of him getting in without taking my keys, and my keys to the school were in my handbag.

What would have been a twenty-minute walk on a normal day took us an hour and a half. The snow was like nothing I'd ever seen before, or since. Before leaving, we got a long piece of rope from the barn and tied it around each of our waists so we couldn't lose each other.

As we reached the main village, we found many of the locals desperately shovelling snow away from their doors. Our pressure lamps had long run out and died by this time, so light from the houses in the village helped us to see our way. As we passed the home of Jenn's family which was only around the corner from the school, I was surprised to see her mother not her father hard at work shovelling, and knowing Jenn, I would have thought Jenn would have been outside helping.

When she saw me, she cried out, stumbling over the snow to hug me. 'Judith, thank God you're here. They need you at the school.'

'What's happening at the school?' I asked, hugging her as she was clearly emotional.

'Earlier this afternoon there was a man knocked on our door for help and told us there was a child it the school. One of the windows was broken, and they were inside. Jenn and her father went for help with a few others to try and find him, but that was three hours ago, and I've not heard a thing since.'

'We're on our way up there now. Have you seen Tommy anywhere? He's missing.'

'I'm sorry.' She yelled over the wind. 'I know he's your son, Jerrold, but I honestly cannot say that I know what he looks like.'

'Don't worry Mrs Brooks?' I told her, 'We'll get up there as fast as we can and see if we can find Jenn and PC Brooks.'

When we finally reached the school, we found more villagers at work with shovels and pressure lanterns. They'd been working hard to clear the doorway of snow. Among the workers were John, the school caretaker, and his son, Joseph, the kitchen assistant and Jenn's would be boyfriend.

PC Brooks was leading the operation, but there was something panicked about him. He wasn't his normal laid-back self. In the light of the gas lamp, I could see tears in his eyes.

'What is it?' I asked him. 'Why are you crying? Where is Jenn? Have any of you seen Tommy?'

'There was a girl in the school.' He trembled, 'We could all hear her yelling through the broken window. God only knows how she got in there, but there was no way to get the doors open without digging. Jenn was the smallest. She climbed up to have a look in the window to calm the girl down and help her.' He wiped his eyes. 'You know our Jenn, she's only a slight little thing. She leaned in the window to yell to the girl, and she fell headfirst. Others went up to call for them, but we've heard nothing since. Not a sound from either of them.'

With that news, I picked up a spare shovel, and I started digging. Only the last of the snow needed clearing. There were tears in my eyes too now. I was terrified that we had already lost little Tommy for good, and from what PC Brooks said, Jenn could be badly hurt or even worse, dead.

Victorian schools in Britain were built with high ceilings and windows. The windows were usually around five feet, but the window she fell through was more like eight feet. There was a hard floor under it. If she fell head-first she could've broken her neck or cracked her skull or something.

The door was soon clear, and I had to turn the key in the lock. There was a cheer as it opened the first time. I was the first to step inside. Jerrold came next, and then offered his hand to help PC Brooks down from the snow into the cleared path.

There was a horrible moment where two of the people climbing down slid and fell against the wall of snow. My heart nearly burst out of my chest with fright as the wall of snow wobbled but held fast.

'Don't scare me like that.' I breathed, but I spoke too soon.

A small piece fell from the pile of snow, not enough to hurt anyone, but it caused a vibration, and the vibration shook the snow on the roof. There was an awful moment when Jerrold and I looked at each other, and there was nothing I could do. There were several tons of snow falling from the roof, and there was no way any of the people were going to avoid being crushed. The was a sudden puff and rumble as a deathly freezing cloud of white came down, and I was knocked off my feet.

Alone in the dark

'Jerrold!' I yelled, 'John, Joe, Sarah, PC Brooks. There was nothing, not an answer from any of them. I called again and again, but there was nothing. The snowdrift left by what fell from the roof covered the door and had spread down the corridor, and blocked the inner door, which was the entry to the lower school, the room where Jenn fell.

I would have to unlock several inner doors to get to her. Thankfully, the light switch was not covered by the drift. I felt for it in the dark and clicked it on. Then I clicked it again and again, but there was no light, nothing, except pitch black. Calling out for Jenn and Tommy, I slid along the wall, heart thumping like mad in my chest.

I reached the door to the small room next to the office which was called the library. It wasn't a library, it was just a bookshelf, but for the children, it was a library.

It took me several minutes to find the right key in the dark. As I turned the lock, I was cursing John and Joe for their insistence on locking every door without any real need to. I heard a noise from the hallway, and it sounded like loud groaning as though a person was hurt or being tortured.

The situation didn't hit me until I reached the next inner door. I was in pitch black in the same building where I had witnessed a typewriter typing a letter on its own. Where desks had been turned upside down and where the ghost of a girl had been. Although the typed letter from the ghost had congratulated me on the job, I was not sure the ghost was friendly. I was, in fact, quite sure that it wasn't.

Where did Maria fit into this? In the dreams, I saw her mainly as a charming, friendly, poor, mentally challenged child, and yet, she could get angry and violent. She hit her grandmother. I felt the anger coursing through her. If she was like that as a child, what was she like as a ghost? What was she capable of and why did Tommy come here to the school. Tommy had said that his ghost M was warning me that the photograph would put me in danger. I should have got rid of it

Suddenly a voice made me jump out of my skin. It came from my handbag. 'Judith.'

'Who said that?'

'Me in here. I can hear your thoughts. I am no am a bad girl. I am a friend of Judith and Jerrold and Thomas and Jerry.'

'Maria, is that you in there?'

'I sorry, Judith, I had to make you come,' said the voice.

There was another noise like someone being tortured from the other side of the door. I fumbled with the keys once more. If only I could get to the office, we had candles in there to use in the event of a power cut.

Finally, I got the middle door open and moved into the office. The voice in my handbag kept on at me, calling, 'Judith, Judith. Please listen. I am a friend. Tommy in danger, you in danger.'

'Maria, I want to believe you, but you are a talking picture of a dead girl. I'm crazy. You're a voice in my head. I need to be taken to the lunatic asylum like Vicky Ashworth. I don't want to end up dead like her.'

'I did no kill Vicky.' She whimpered. 'She, my friend. She ill in the head. I try befriend before she goes crazy.'

I finally got into the office and felt in the drawer for a candle. I had matches in my pocket and lit up one of the candles. At least now there was a small ball of light in front of me.

Bang... the drawer of the desk slammed. I shrieked out in terror.

Strangely the voice in my bag screamed too.

'What the hell are you screaming for, Maria?' I demanded.

'Because I'm as scared of the ghost as you are!'

'You are the ghost!' I replied, getting frustrated at these voices in my head. I had talked to her before, and I had thought I heard her reply, or I would make up something I thought she would say, but now she was talking to me like we were having a real conversation.

'I am not a ghost.' She shrieked, 'I do not know what I am, but no ghost.'

'Who is it then, if it's not you?' I trembled.

'Bad, a bad, bad man who Kathleen married and made her become Judith.'

'Edward? But why here? Why now? And why can you talk now?'

'To use the power, I have to suck up energy. I can no d-do at you home b-because sad lonely place has little happiness. You are always sad and lonely, but school is happy place. You happy here, you and Jenn, Dave Robinson. You made this place buzz and it makes me work better.'

'Like a giant battery of emotion.' I breathed, 'Tommy told us that his ghost explained about the power of the school. She needs it for him to see her.'

'That right.'

'So, at my house, you can't talk, so you try to move things like matches.'

'Yes'

'But why did you keep writing hell with my matches.'

I could swear I heard her start to cry. I took out the photo and held it to the light. Sure enough, there was a tear in her eye.

'It no my fault I can no spell fast enough. They would no let me go to school because I am the village idiot.'

'What were you trying to say, Maria?'

'The girl in the picture sniffed. 'I wanted to say hello. The first time I could not spell fast. Then I try again but not enough matches because you smoke too much.'

'I could do with a smoke right now.' I sighed.

Bang went the desk once more.

'That all you got ghost?' I screamed, coming out of the office to where the folding doors separated the main hall from the lower school where Jenn had fallen. 'You must have something scarier than that you coward.'

I shouldn't have said that. Suddenly all of the glass windows in the dividing wall came crashing down and shattered all over the floor.

'I'm sorry I thought you did this.' I breathed.

'Everyone always blames me for everything.' She squealed, just like the angry-wronged child that she was. 'It's not fair Granna blames me for everything, so other people frightened. I am not a ghost. I am a good, nice, friendly girl, but nobody likes me because I am not clever. 'I am so, so sorry Maria, but do you know what he plans to do?'

'He saw you.' She squealed, 'He saw you cheating on him with Jerrold, so he wants to kill Tommy. He will kill Jerrold then you.'

'How do you know this, Maria?' I questioned, struggling with the door in the folding wall, hoping to get to the next divider where Jenn should be on the other side, and I could find out if she was alive.

'You put me on your desk next to his photograph. He is not as old as me, and only the power of this place brought him to life, like the power of Maria's thoughts, and her pain brought me to life. He is evil, and he is angry, and he has Tommy.'

Finally, the door swung open, and I moved on to the next one. There was the rumbling groaning sound again. There were noises on the other side of the second partition wall. I tried to shout for Jenn, but more stuff was banging around. I was suddenly being pelted with textbooks and pencils and all sorts of objects.

Surely, they were figments of my imagination because of the hypothermia.

When the last door flung open, I stood there catching my breath, when out of nowhere this sheet appeared at the edge of the ball of light. It was moving towards me at speed and seeing as the school was haunted and ghosts in my mind look like sheets floating the air, I decided to run.

I made it through both of the partition doors and across the hallway and was fiddling with the door of my new classroom. I could hear the ghost getting closer and closer, and I could swear it was calling my name as it got closer and closer. 'Judith, Judith, come back.'

Suddenly there was a hand on my back, and I shrieked out loud, thinking of my impending death.

'Judith it's okay it's me.'

'Jenn,' I screamed, hugging her. 'They said you had fallen. I thought you were dead.'

'Nope.' She grinned, 'Lucky I forgot to put the dressing-up clothes away yesterday, and I landed on the pile.

'But there was a strange noise, like somebody was being tortured in that room, and there was a white sheet floating, so I thought it was a ghost and I ran.'

'Did the cloth you saw look like this.' She held it up for me to see. I nodded, feeling stupid. 'Ha ha.' she grinned, 'You're scared of my hanky, whhooooooo. Ah ah ah eeehhh eehh aaaacchhhhoooooo.'

Then she blew her nose so loud that it echoed around the large empty room like a person crying in pain.

'That would be the torturing sound then.' I smiled. 'Where did you get such a nasty cold.'

She turned to me with a sarcastic look.

'It might have been because a crazy woman with a snotty cold kissed me the other morning when I was trying to sleep.'

'Good point' I almost laughed, 'But more importantly have you seen Tommy?'

'Tommy?' She shrugged. 'I thought we were looking for a girl that was in the window.'

'You mean M,' said a voice from my hand.

'Who said that?' She shrieked.

'Brace yourself.' I told her, holding up the photograph.

• • •

'HEY, JENN' She smiled, waving.

Jenn fainted.

The other photograph

I opened the door to my new classroom, holding a very faint Jenn in my other arms. I explained what had happened outside with the snowdrift collapsing on Jerrold, Joe, Jerry and PC Brooks. Jenn swore a told me she hoped they were okay.

'Tommy' I yelled, the second I opened the door, but there was no reply. 'Tommy,' I called and suddenly my heart leapt.

'Judith,' Came a small voice from the other end of the room.

'Tommy, sweetheart, what are you doing here?'

'Aunty Judith, you need to go.' Tommy called. 'He wants to kill you.'

'Who has you?'

'I have him, Kathleen,' said a voice that seemed to come from the very walls. A voice that I thought I would never hear again.

'Edward.' I breathed. What the hell? All this time, I was blaming the spirit of Maria or Tommy's friendly ghost for everything that was going on at the school, and all the time it was the ghost of my former husband following me around.

'Kathleen, I'm going to make you pay for what you've done.'

Things started crashing down from the ceiling and desks were flying across the room. I ducked for cover, my heart pounding.

'You created me, Kathleen. While Edward was away, you talked to me. You poured your heart to me as if I was him and you made me come alive, and now you don't even look at me.'

'Who on earth is this man and what is he talking about?' Jenn gasped as she struggled for breath.

'It would seem it's the ghost of my ex-husband and he kidnapped Tommy.'

'Thank you for the advice,' I replied, ducking as a flying desk missed me by inches. 'But you are a picture of a dead girl and that makes you a ghost.'

'I am no a ghost.' She argued back as Jenn and I crawled towards the other end of the room still looking for the ghost of Edward. 'I don't know what, but am no the ghost Maria. I am not her. Just like that is not him. I am no a ghost of Maria, because she is not dead '

'He no a ghost he's like me he is like me.' Came Maria's voice.

'I'm sorry I think she died years ago' I told over the howling of the wind.

'No it' It cried, 'She just went out to see farther she's coming back.'

There was not time to digest what she as without warning the crashing and banging stopped dead. You could here a pin drop. I took my opportunity to stand up and run forward to the end of the classroom where I had heard Tommy yelling from. I searched around yelling,

'Tommy, where are you?'

'Tommy, Tommy, where are you?' Edward's voice mocked. 'Judith, Judith, I'm over here.' Came his voice from different locations. 'The snotty little brat was never here.' He cackled.

'I might not have the boy, but now I have you trapped.' The desks shot up into the air and stayed there for a second in the pitch black before forming a circle in the air and crashing down around me to make a cage of sorts.

They were piled high, but it was very easy for me to just slide out between the legs.

'Damn and blast!' I heard Edward yell.

'Why are you doing this, Edward?' I yelled into the dark. 'And why now?'

The very walls of the building started to tremble. 'You cheated on me, you bitch.'

'I did no such thing,' I replied into the dark. 'Marriage is until death do us part. You died, and you weren't even a good husband. Me sleeping with Jerrold has nothing to do with you.'

'Oh my God,' Jenn screamed, from the other side of the room.

'Are you okay, Jenn?' I called.

'Yes,' she replied, 'But, you're sleeping with Jerrold. That's the best news I've heard in weeks. I'm gonna have to tell… Erm, I won't tell anyone.' She promised.

'I'm not talking about Jerrold. I'm talking about that snotty little halfwit girl in the photograph.'

'Maria. You're jealous about my mad rambling to a photograph of a disabled child.'

'He's been bullying me for months.' Maria shrieked. 'Each time you go out for lunch or break time, he comes to life like me, but he says horrible things and makes me cry, because you like me and you never talked to him anymore.'

'Maybe because you're an asshole and you beat me up.'

'For years while the real Edward was at war, I was there for you.' He bellowed. 'He was off fighting in the war, and you lay in bed at night talking to me as if I was him. You poured your heart and soul into talking to me, just like the halfwit girl did to the photo of herself.'

Just then a piece of debris hit the lamp in my hand and shattered it, spreading paraffin all over the floor and it burned. The bits of broken desk on the floor were set alight.

'Wait, so you're not Edward, you're just the photograph of him.'

'Does it matter what I am now that I've got you?' He bellowed. 'You went home, and you took the girl home. I was here alone, all night and all day, and I used the opportunity to suck in more of the power of this place. I controlled the boy and made him come to find me, and I would use my powers. I have already killed Jerrold, and now it's your…'

'Judith, Tommy, are you in here?' came Jerrold's voice.

'I think he might be lying about killing Jerrold.' Jenn laughed out loud.

'We're in here, but we can't find Tommy, but I got Jenn here,' I called.

Seconds later, Jerrold, Jerry, John, Joe and PC Brooks, joined Jenn and me in the classroom. It was a case of spot the person whose name didn't begin with J.

'A hha ha. ' The voice boomed from around the room. 'Now you are all here, you can witness the violent death of J…'

'Got him!' Jenn shouted excitedly. 'She ran into the light of the fire holding up the small photograph of my husband which I had left on my desk.

'Let me go you brat.' He boomed, 'Unwanted basted child I see the sinful thoughts in your head, I see your desires to lay with other women.'

'No, I'm going to give you to Judith, and she can do what she wants with you. Right after I a-a-a ahh a*chhhhewww*!'

She quite deliberately sneezed all over the face of the picture. She laughed as Mucous ran all over him.

'You are a disgusting child' He bellowed through the glass of his wooden prison frame.

'Wait.' He yelled as Jenn was about to pass him to me. 'I can tell you who your father is.'

'Oh, the big reveal moment.' She smiled, laughing. 'Well, you might as well know everyone because I do.'

She passed the photograph to me. 'I'm sure it isn't going to come as much of a surprise that Mr Robinson was my father.'

Thank god she knew so I didn't have to tell her.

'From Judith's reaction, she already knew and wasn't going to tell me.' She smiled adding, 'But I'm angry with you for not telling me so you don't talk to me for at least 5 minutes……Oh forget it hug me.'

I think she underestimated the huge gasp that would arise from this news. The whole room was in shock.

'My mother worked at the school' she sighed telling those gathered. 'You all know she not very tall and she looks young just like I do, but she was nineteen and a consenting adult when I was conceived. She had to leave her job when she had me because she wasn't married and it was thought she would bring shame upon the school and the headmaster would have lost job if people found out.

I remembered the words had been spread on the flaw in ink. 'The headmaster Fucked Children' That had just been a rumour because Jenn's mother looked like a child at the time. So my uncle might wasn't a paedophile.

'He was good man and looked after and mum even after things ended and you came along didn't he father .' She smiled sadly at PC Brooks who must have known this all and he nodded in agreement.

'Kathleen…' Edward's voice boomed. 'If you harm me, I will tell everyone who you really are what you did and why you changed your name.'

He must have thought that was something that bothered me. What he didn't realise was that while everyone was in shock over Jenn's revelation, I was sliding the card out of its frame. Without a word, I calmly tore him into quarters and threw him in the fire. He burned, and I never saw or heard from him again.

Mary

There was a loud bang, and the side room which led to the cloakroom burst open. A little hand appeared through the door shaking with cold.

'Tommy.' Jerrold and I cried at the same time.

'Dad and Aunty Judith,' he smiled. 'A bad man made me come here, but M put me in the cloakroom and kept me safe.

There were gasps of shock all around when a girl who looked about twelve followed him out of the door.

'Mary!' Jerry screamed, 'My Mary.'

She was three or four years older, there stood the girl who had brought the photograph of Maria to the school twenty years before.

That was why the school ghost hung around Tommy, of course. She was Tommy's mother.

We always thought by M he meant Maria, but it was M for Mary.

'I can't stay long.' She whispered, as though she was a breath on the wind. 'He drained all the energy from this place. 'Judith,' she breathed. 'Thank you for looking after Tommy in my absence. You and Jerrold have my blessing. You will go on to have more children, but stop smoking because in a few years they will find out it causes cancer and I don't want Tommy or Jerrold losing anyone else.'

Mary changed in front of us from a child into the young woman she had been at the time of her death.

'Jerrold' She groaned, 'I Will always love you, but death did us part and Judith is your mate, not me. These things are just meant to be.'

She then turned to Jerry, but we could see her light and energy fading. The photo of Maria had quietened too, as though she had just run out of power.

Tommy came running and hugged his dad and me.

'Father,' she whispered, 'Maria is not dead. She was released from prison and put in an asylum after nobody collected her.'

She then turned to Jenn. 'Jenn, you know Maria, you just don't know that you know her.'

With that, she disappeared like.

Jenn's eyes were wide open. 'Maria Smith'

'You know her, Jenn?'

'I i I' she stuttered. ' I don't know let me think…... Hang on! Yes I think I do.'

There was an intake of breath. 'Thorpe Mental Hospital where I visited Victoria Ashworth before she topped herself. What would she be? In fifties?'

'Yes, yes, she would.' Jerry breathed pausing with tears in his gleaming. 'Yes.' He breathed she'd be Fifty two.

'I do know her!.' She shouted excitedly as Jerry started to cry. 'She was in one of the rooms down the hallway from Victoria, and she just kept saying Jay will come to get me, but the nurses were horrible to her and they mocked her and told her nobody was coming. Jenn paused. 'They said she was in prison for murder. Is that true?'

• • •

'It's true,' Jerry nodded. 'She blamed my father for everything because she was too mentally young to understand it wasn't his fault. One day he had enough, and he attacked his daughter out on the farm. There was a struggle and he was hit on the head with a pitchfork to bring him out of his rage and stop him from hurting Maria. Only he was hit too hard and it killed him.' He breathed. 'It was me. I hit him to get him off her, but with no intention of causing real harm. His injuries were so bad they would never believe it hadn't been intentional.

'The old bugger died, and I was the only one who could keep the family farm going with my young siblings to feed, while Maria couldn't do anything to pull her weight. So, Mother and Gran shopped her to the police and told them she hit my father. They thought she would get off because of her disability, but no such luck. She was sent down for twenty years and went to a prison in Lincolnshire so far away that we couldn't visit easily in those days'

'Jenn you told me the day we met there was a murder on the camping field thirty years ago' I breathed as Jerry wiped tears of joy from his face. It made sense now, the words on the scrabble bored. Surely It was manslaughter not murder but either way Jerry would have gone to jail and his family might have sarved. I thought this was very hard on Maria. I would later come to the conclusion that the photograph didn't show me these things because everythying she showed me came from memories that the real Maria had before she was photographed or she transferred to her when she talked.

'I guess she never saw the photograph again after what happened.' I asked Jerry who shook his head.'She ran away into the forest after I hit him. The police found her a few hours later and took her away. She was held in Norwich but the last time I saw her was in court in 1917. The jury saw she wasn't like others and took mercy on her by avoiding hanging her. ' He sobbed,' Gran and Grandad died a year later and mother soon after. I just assumed that she died because we never heard anything from the prison. I couldn't even have told you what one she was in. let alone that she'd been released.' He took a deep breath as tears of joy ran don his face into his beard.

It was a yell from PC Brooks that brought Jerry's tail to a halt. So engrossed were we all in the story we'd forget the school was on fire and it need putting out.

Epilogue added in 2017

Much of the story you've just read was completed on an old typewriter in the years after I retired after many years at Hevingham School. After many years of gathering dust in a draw, my granddaughter has typed it for me on a computer and put it out on the worldwide web for all to see. Here I wish to add some things that happened in the years that followed up to 2019.

In the great circle of life, we don't make it to the end at the same time. Some of us pass before our time, and some like me have a long life. In January 2020, when I reach the big one hundred, and get my letter from the Queen, it will be a celebration of my life, but to me it will be a sad day. A day in which we remember all those who've passed over. Considering the events of this story happened so long ago, practically everyone is gone, apart from me.

As planned, Jenn went on to teaching college and became a fully qualified teacher. There was no job space at that time for her to re-join the staff at Hevingham primary school. Still, she returned to the village and commuted on her bicycle to her job in one of the neighbouring village schools in Buxton.

She and Joe remained friends, but she made it clear to him she was not romantically interested, and she gave up her trips to the cinema insisting that he took Suzy who she had previously tried to prevent him taking. Despite being Joe's second choice, he married Suzy and had three children.

Also, since our accidental kiss and Jenn's apparent enjoyment of it I remain convinced that Jenn was a lesbian or bisexual. (Both of which were sadly illegal back then. She would go on to marry an estate agent called Richard Brownlow. In retirement, she finally visited all the places she told me she wanted to go to all those years ago. Over new year 2007-08 her whole family including in-laws, apart from her youngest grandson, went to Australia. While they were on route back to the UK, their plane hit trouble and crashed into the sea. All on board were lost, that included Jenn's four-year-old great-granddaughter. The 'Young Jenn' as I still called her was seventy-eight years old. Her only remaining grandson Robert and his lovely wife Kat still visit me often.

Sometimes in life, we took risks because they made us happy at the time. Making love with a parent of one of my school children could be classed a risk even nowadays, let alone seventy-plus years ago. Things moved quickly and Jerrold and I were married before anyone guessed I was up the duff with his child. I married Jerrold, and with the help of a substitute teacher, some very understanding governors, and family and friends, I managed to have a family and went on to remain headmistress of the school. I remained in the post forty more years, finally retiring aged sixty and a grandma many times over. I passed the job of head teacher to a lovely man called Mr Langmead who looked after Maria's photograph for me continuing her legend.

My second marriage was much happier than my first. Jerrold and I spend our autumn years travelling. Jerold passed away in 2010 aged ninety.

Maria, the real one, was right where Jenn had met her nearly a year earlier. She served twenty years for the murder she did not commit and was then in the asylum for another 10 years. All the years that Jerry thought his sister was dead she'd been in an asylum just outside of Norwich. After all the time I spent with her photograph, the real Maria had no idea who I was, but when she saw her brother after Thirty years, the again jumped out of her chair, and cried for an hour before telling the nurses. 'Told you Jay was coming!'

Now you want to know why I changed my name. Well, it's simple. When my husband died the house that his parents bought him went to me in the will. They tried to contest the will, but I'd already sold the house and banked the money. So, I changed my name and moved to somewhere they wouldn't find me.

When Maria came out of that asylum, I remembered she had wanted to see the world. New York and Paris. How Jerry said he would take her one day. With no need to spend the money on another house, I used it to finance family holidays to all of the places that Maria thought she would never see.

Maria lived for many more years. One day when she was Seventy-years-old, she sat in her boat, the HMS Maria, and she lay back and looked at the sun, then fell asleep for the last time.

As for the photograph and how it came to be. I believed that it was something rarely seen in this world. A young, troubled, mentally challenged girl poured her heart and soul into that photograph, so much so that it took on a life and soul of its own. Then, when she was gone, the photo tried to find friends of her own.

I went on to be the headmistress of Hevingham School for thirty years, retiring in 1980. During this time I was able to keep my job while having three children with Jerrold two girls and a boy. I passed the job of headteacher to a lovely fellow called Mr Langmead. I told him about Maria and how I wanted her photograph to stay in the school where she was happy. He continued her tale for many students in his time there.

Ten years after I retired when Mr Langmead himself retired, she was again left at the school, where she was happy around the children, but soon after he left there were rumours of disturbances at the school and she was blamed, so then the new headmaster threw her in the bin, and she was never seen or heard from again.

Well, that's the official story. The unofficial one is that I crept up to the school in the dead of night and stole her back.

Thomas still lives on the farm but it's his grandchildren that keep it running for him. A far smaller business than in it's heyday.

I Due to old age and failing health, I no longer live in the village I grew to love. The last time I visited the school was for my great-grandaughter's leavers assembly in 2016. From the road it looks the same as it did forty years ago with the headmaster's cottage long demolished and the gateway bricked up. However the back and inside of the school have modernised so much that I no longer recognise it. As Evan Benton, (A local collector of memories) once said in his book "A man and boy in a Norfolk vlillage." Hevingham to me now has become a village of strangers. I was once one of those strangers and to many I still am. People come and go. People are born and they die. But the people who are gone live long in the memories of those who love and remember them.

So, I shall be one hundred years old in January 2020. I now live in a nursing home, where I plan to die quite soon, with any luck, but for now, I shall be known as the crazy old lady who talks to her photograph.

THE END

To this day although many of the people involved are either no longer with us or unwilling to talk I have not given up hope of finding t out the truth about the real photograph.

Also By Samuel J White

A MIDWINTER NIGHT'S DREAM: THE BROCCOLI, THE STILTON AND THE HAYSTACK.

Lonely teenage fitness instructor Rob meets immigrant caravan cleaner Katarzyna wandering in a blizzard. But after a bizarre set of circumstances, they find themselves asleep, together with no dry clothes sheltering from the storm. Rob has strange dreams about Katarzyna which he'd rather not disclose just yet. Rob is fascinated to discover that she has experienced a similar dream to match his. Continuing to dream of a future the pair are left to wonder what is really going on. Are they really there at the beginning of something new or watching their vivid memories flash before them as they die? Or is something more complex and sinister occurring? Immerse yourself in this tale of mesmerizing dreams, bold ghosts and angels. With a real deep love that is so complex even they can't fathom the true nature of it.

http://mybook.to/Amwnd2019edit

This author needs to be picked up by a big publisher. This story was emotionally turbulent. I laughed so hard I cried and cried so hard I had to blow my nose. I can't wait to read his other books!!!

Keri Kankovsky 5 stars

This is an interesting read that is a bit of a romance with a few other genres thrown into the mix. When Rob helps a young woman named Kat during a blizzard on a midwinter night, things I never expected happen and the story unfolds. I like the

author's writing style and the laid back way this story is told. I think this author is one to keep an eye on.
P.S.Winn 4 stars

DERAILED AND DISPERSED 4 Part series

In 1999 A group of colleagues are travelling on a train across the Norfolk Marshes when it crashes leaving people injured and missing. With no phone signal, the group splits up to get help only to find themselves in a new nightmare witch, ghost vampire and werewolves and the very fate of the world is in their hands.

http://mybook.to/DAD1

Roaring into the sunset 2020

In the split second before they feel the impact of their possible impending doom. The lives of the adrenaline junky couple Dave and Sarah flash before their eyes. But after all their struggles will their lives end this way? Or can they stop it? A twisting, warming, humourous, yet heartwrenching, coming-of age-tale. Told by both Dave and Sarah set in the backdrop of the '80s and 90s East Anglia.
(Some scenes themes of violence and attitudes which belong in the past.
The author takes his readers on an interesting and wonderful journey with the main characters in such a way it feels as though you know them personally. I enjoyed this novel immensely. I would highly recommend this literary masterpiece to anyone and everyone. Tenisha Milla 2022 five stars.